ME-TIME TALES

Tea breaks for mature women and curious men

ROSALIND MINETT

A catalogue record of this book is available
from the British Library
ISBN 978-0-9927167-9-0

Uptake publications: Kingswood Manor
Cottage, Surrey, KT20 7AJ

DEDICATION

In loving memory of Alex,
prince of quirky

CONTENTS

UNDERWHELMED

Marian took stock of her fifty-year-old self when she was only forty-five. It meant wearing support knickers and a suggestive smile. It meant thinking positive, just as she advised her sales colleagues every day. Cerise was her positive colour and she let collars or scarves of it peep out from behind her grey coat, navy mac or black fleecy. She kept her eyes wide open, wide enough, she thought.

She met Pete in the park, walking his dog. It was a tattered specimen with a square head and pus-rimmed eyes. She'd never been into dogs, really, but it was a way of meeting people.

'Hello, boy!' She bent and patted him gingerly. She had wet-wipes in her bag.

Its owner stood up straighter, and he was quite tall, quite amenable with no sign of a beer gut or sustainable reading matter. He tweaked the lead. 'I think he likes you. He's smiling.'

'That's nice. Nice boy.' She left it at that, no kissy noises.

'I'm Pete.' He took the lead off and the dog minced a few paces.

'Oh. Hi.' She smoothed her hair. 'I'm Marian. I'll throw his ball if you like.' She managed to lob it as far as the trees where she hoped he'd find other doggie friends to keep him occupied. The dog ran to it, but not very fast so she had time to look at the man and smile.

He wore a North Face sweat shirt with no stains down the front, and the gingery colour matched his eyes. Perhaps he'd had ginger hair once, like she'd had this really fair hair herself when she was little. People would say, 'What a little angel'. But that was a long time ago, further off than the dog in the woodland patch.

'He's run a long way, bless him.'

'He'll come back.' He smiled and showed all his teeth, definitely real. 'I see you like dogs.'

She nodded and opened her coat a touch.

He said, 'It's good to meet a fellow spirit. I don't meet enough people who like dogs.'

'No? They should do. I do.'

'Nice one, Mary—'

'Marian!'

'Marian, sure,' he said, looking at her Nike trainers, and when the dog ran back, they walked round the park together. She'd known that pink-edged footwear was worth the extra money.

At home on the fourth floor in her studio flat that looked out on to the fourth floor of the next block, Marian made herself an instant cappuccino from a sachet. It tasted a bit metallic.

She could meet Pete in a café for cappuccinos if he didn't have the dog.

It was cold the next day, but she thought she'd take a turn round the park after work. She could warm up with a hot chocolate and a donut when she got home.

She recognised the dog at a distance, from his run, the way his back paws showed their fluffy bits as they kicked up. His master was wrapped in a maroon and navy scarf. Rather like an old school uniform scarf, but of course it couldn't be; they didn't last that long. She walked nearer, careful to take no notice.

She saw from the sudden upwards jerk of his hand that Pete remembered her. So did the dog, who rushed up willingly. This time his ball was covered in goo from his mouth, so she didn't offer to throw it.

She said casually, 'Oh. Hallo again. Pete, isn't it? I'm just walking to the pond.'

Pete followed her, putting the dog on the lead when they neared the ducks. It was quite a long walk and ended culturally as there was an exhibition in the glass-sided building at the far end. The paintings were abstract but colourful.

'After all,' Pete said interestingly, 'if they were actual *pictures*, the council would be too scared about theft to exhibit them here.'

'I suppose so, but it would be nice to recognise something— like a cup or a tree. Still, I like this one, sort of spotty and stripy, with those maroon patches. It reminds me of your scarf.'

He looked at her with kind eyes. 'Good of you to notice. They are similar hues, I agree.'

'The dog's getting restless, should we go?'

'So thoughtful, putting the dog first. He can sense you really care.'

The weeks passed. Even when it rained, Marian went to the park saying 'Just on my way home from work.'

She would see Pete wandering around or sitting in the glass place if it was pouring. He didn't seem to work. He'd described himself as a man of independent means, so that meant he didn't have to work, she supposed.

'It's nice that you're always here when I am.'

'Dogs have to be walked, so I'm always here.'

There was a refreshment stall at the western gate that was sometimes open.

'Could you do with a coffee?' he asked, after they had met on sufficient occasions. He wasn't too forward.

The stall didn't sell cappuccinos and the cups were cardboard with an extra cardboard ring to stop you burning your hands. Pete paid, so she knew he was a decent sort of guy even if he took three sugars and put one sachet in his pocket.

'Oh, thank you,' she said, perching on a nearby litter bin. 'This is very welcome. I do love a coffee.'

The dog sniffed at her legs, which was annoying.

'He can't leave you alone.'

'No,' and she gave out a giggle. He was probably too shy to mean it was Pete himself who couldn't.

It turned out that this wasn't to be the only time he treated her to a coffee at the stall. Soon the dog made a bee-line for it, showing an expectation that they would all be hovering there for deliciously smelly moments.

Eventually, Marian put it to Pete that they met so often they were *going out together*.

'Yes. Me, you and the dog. We're park regulars. He's getting dependent on seeing you.'

She took this as a metaphor for his own feelings and later that week bought herself a cerise jumper in mohair. The time would come when she wouldn't be buying her own jumpers.

In fact, Pete wasn't the kind of boy-friend who gave endearments or little gifts until Marian told him what to do.

'Right, and now we're regular, you know, on my birthday it would be nice to get a card. "With all my love, Pete." That sort of thing.' And on her birthday she got a card. "To Marian, all my love, Pete." It had a parrot on it, and a jungle scene behind it.

'You remembered! Thank you, Pete.'

'I have to know what's expected,' he explained, but he didn't put the expected hand in his inside pocket. There was nothing to draw out. For a man of independent means he seemed mean.

She shoved her hands round her own waist. 'It's no good you just meeting me in the park with that raggedy dog.' She had shocked him, she could see, but she went on, 'Well, we can't walk round forever, talking about not very much, can we? And it's me doing the talking, because you don't talk much, do you, Pete?'

'If I've got anything interesting to say, I will. I promise.'

'Go on then.'

He talked about things he knew: cylinder valves, UFOs, micro-organisms and sprockets. 'There's a lot of variety in my life-style.'

She shouldn't have pressed him. She tried to stimulate the conversation, trying colours, natural disasters, television personalities, and finally, dog breeds. He didn't know many of those, which surprised her.

6

They went out together for over a year. The dog too.

On Valentine's Day, Pete bought Marian four red roses, a card saying "All my love, Pete," and a bargain pack of Mars bars. It was more or less what she'd asked for the week before and the week before that. A box of chocolates was what she'd actually said, hoping for one with a bow, Belgian perhaps. But she hadn't stated that categorically.

'I should do something for you,' she said. 'I don't want you thinking I'm one of those women who take, take, take.'

'No,' he said, thoughtfully. 'Yes. Well, you could make me a promise.'

She drew in her breath sharply and her left hand from its mitten.

'There's something I want you to look after for me . . .'

'Oh. Okay then. When?'

'Sometime. Will you promise?'

'I promise,' she said in sincere mode, her left hand resting lightly on the back of the park bench. His grandmother had died not long ago. Perhaps it was his grandmother's ring he wanted her to care for, an antique of great sentimental value. Not something to entrust with any old girl-friend.

Perhaps that was why he'd never got engaged before.

As the weeks drew emptily by, she thought the reason he'd kept her waiting, her Pete, for such a long time, was to be sure, really sure. Or maybe he was saving up. Christmas was expensive after all. He'd bought her a food mixer, a silky camisole and a personalised card, all according to her precise suggestion.

She bought him a new dog lead and collar in lavender blue. She couldn't think what else would appeal to him.

It wasn't until the end of January, the wind so bitter and the ground so lethal with ice that she wouldn't risk the walk with the mangy dog, and Pete agreeing the weather was too terrible for walking a dog and how he hated it, that talk of the Caribbean occurred.

When she telephoned, he said he wished he was in the Caribbean, and she said that would be idyllic (lovely word). Was he planning a wonderful surprise, that man of few words?

She let him know she had her passport up to date. She had been to Marbella the summer before she met him, but got horribly sun-burned.

As February began, the weather was even worse, so cold and miserable they hadn't seen each other for ten days. She had a bad cold, so didn't push herself to go to work. There was an omnibus edition of Neighbours, so she was all right. Marian planned to explore the sales when the weather eventually improved. Royal blue could prove a faster-moving colour than cerise. But the weather stayed, as irresolute as a padlock. She watched repeat programmes, wrapped in a blanket.

Then an email arrived with a photograph attachment; an azure scene from the Caribbean.

Much better here, Marian, glad to say! I'm as bronze as a gas boiler. The Caribbean is definitely for me. I'm staying put. I've given up the tenancy of my flat from the end of the month.

Remember that promise you gave me? I'm really grateful to you. Just look after the dog, that's all. It's been a real burden to me, Gran's inheritance.

I left my keys with Will, next door. He's holding the fort, but the dog will be glad to see you for his walks and pats. Best let him move in with you, permanently. I know how lucky I am to have found someone who will really care for him.

Have fun,

All my love,

Pete.'

When she'd finished screaming silently to herself and growling at the computer screen that still displayed the vivid sea and tropical verbiage, Marian checked her appearance in the mirror. Was she only worth nurturing as a dog walker? Was cerise really her colour? She tore off the little spotted scarf softening the neckline of her navy twinset and donned a sensible mac and lace-up shoes. No point dressing up for a dog.

It was true, the dog did appear delighted to see her, and Will, relieved. He met her with a wide-open door and lifted eyebrows as well as a smile. At least she counted for something.

'Pete thought a lot of you, Marian, you know.' The implication was that he was dead already, at least to her. 'Really considerate and reliable he said you were.'

'Mm. Right.'

'Dog's nearly out of dog biscuits but here's a couple of his tins. Go easy on them, he really pongs after he's eaten meat.'

Her eyes dropped to the dog's rear parts and then to Heaven. 'I know.' She swallowed. 'Thanks.'

She took the lead and a plastic carrier with the tins and small remains of biscuit. A trip to the supermarket was obviously going to be her first stop. She set off.

'Wait!' he called.

She stopped, a germ of hope fluttering somewhere under her coat and layers. This Will wasn't a bad-looking guy, if a bit casual in his *Diggers Do It* T-shirt.

He proffered a hand. 'Tut, tut, you haven't taken a little black bag for the whoopsies.'

She took one and shoved it fiercely in her pocket with a nod. It was hard not to seem bad-tempered.

The dog was very well behaved along the High Street. Obviously he didn't want to chance his luck. She caught sight of herself in a shop window. Not smart, not even attractive given the mac and shoes, but purposeful somehow. It wouldn't take much to improve her image, would it?

The dress in the window was a vibrant blue, a gentian shade. *Gentian*. What a civilised name. She tied the dog to a lamp-post and cast him a threatening look. The dress was too ridiculously expensive but there was a rack of scarves, one of them the same colour. She held it to her face opposite the mirror.

'Just your colour!' exclaimed the assistant.

'I'll take it. Thank you.'

Next morning, after his early walk, the dog promised with his eyes to behave while Marian was at work.

Her trainees told her there was something new in her appearance, they admired the blue.

'Gentian,' she said. 'A gentle colour, but a bite to it. It's positive, a definitive statement. In management, everyone, we have to take action but we don't have to be overly aggressive. Now, let's try that presentation again.'

She had to dash home in her lunch break to be on the safe side, but the dog had hardly moved from where she had left him, except a foot higher to the sofa.

Early evening in the park she was nodded to by several other dog owners and approached, via the dog, by a man with a briefcase.

'What a well-mannered dog,' he said, having finished patting him. 'Doesn't jump up. All credit to you.'

His trousers were well creased and his shoes highly polished. Praise from a guy in a suit!

It made something to look forward to after work, the walk. And there were other parks she could take the dog to.

She bought a gentian blouse with pointed collars that poked invitingly out of her coat lapels.

You never know. With a dog, life is full of possibilities.

BLIND DATE

I'm just finishing this flaming ironing. I hate it, I really hate it, but, like, my brother Nick fixed me up with this Mark.

'You'll love him,' he said. 'Just your type.'

'No I shan't, not if you've chosen him.' But fact was, no-one fanciable was trending on my scene at the moment even though my tatts are awesome (vampire, dragon lily) and I'm at my peak: sixteen-and-a-half. I couldn't fake getting off with anyone and I did need a date or two or my street cred would go down the pan. I have the reputation of being well choosy. Didn't want to lose it.

This *Mark* rang me.

I played it cool. 'Sorry? You're who?'

He told me, with a flash of charm. Then he said, 'Where shall we meet?'

'Haven't said I would.'

'What's the harm? Your brother's okayed me, hasn't he? He showed me your selfie on his iPhone. You'll do for me.'

'Yeah. I'm supposed to be flattered?'

He chuckled, (quite a nice sound, not squeaky, not guttural). 'So give it a go. Why not? This Friday night?'

'P'raps. I don't know what you look like, remember. You might be dead geeky.'

'Cheeky.'

I smiled. I couldn't quite stop myself. He couldn't see me, after all. Let him sweat.

His voice went deep brown. 'How should I look then?'

I melted. If only he worked out! 'Haven't thought,' I said.

'I'm not so bad. Try me – or we could skype.'

'Not.' He sounded legend.

'Come on. Give me a go. Yolo.'

I manufactured a sigh. 'Oh— I suppose. Just for a drink. As long as you've got good legs.' I was giggling to myself but I put Mum's J-cloth over the mouthpiece to block the sound. I was joking, but yay, I really do hate a bloke to have fat or thin legs. They're a dead turn-off.

He stopped saying anything.

'What's up?'

'A small detail.'

Whoops, he was serious now, sober. Might think I'm a prat. 'What?'

'I'll explain when I see you. How about 7.30 – Rat and Parrot? Nick will be there and Tony, another mate, so you'll be safe enough.'

I agreed before I could say anything else stupid. I couldn't help wondering if he had great walloping thighs or weak knobbly knees. Why that silence, else?

Nick agreed to go ahead of me on the Friday so that I could come into the pub and see directly who Mark was because they'd be sitting together, facing the door.

I didn't let Nick know how long I took to get ready. I didn't use any bling but I gelled my hair so it sat just right above my ears and on to my shoulders, and at the fourth change I put on the cherry T-shirt that everyone said was exactly my colour. It matched my quiff. My mates all say I've got swag.

I waited till seven forty before I made my entrance, casual like, but swinging my hips. My shorts were bum-hugging and I had these tiger-stripe tights. I looked straight at the bar so that I could wave and smile to Paulo the barman, like I was in there every night, his best customer. But Paulo did recognise me, so that was okay. It was only then that I looked round vaguely as if it hardly mattered whether I spotted Mark or not. He and Nick were right in front of me, in fact, but I deliberately didn't look there.

Nick did his bit. 'Hey, Sis. Over here,' although he'd guess that I already knew and that I was playing it cool.

I turned and looked. My knees turned to water. Sick. Mark's eyes were lush; a green dream, fringed by dark lashes. I tensed my face muscles not to let on I rated him, and forced my eyes to move sideways to the bloke next to him. I wasn't letting Nick see my eyes. He'd detect a glint even if I wore sunglasses.

Nick inclined his head. 'Jess, this is Tony and *this* – he underlined it – is Mark.'

I made myself smile sweetly at Tony with his bad skin and cowboy shirt. (Poor bloke, body okay, face butters). Why should Mark get to think I was up for it? Why should Nick get to think he was right?

'Right, Tony?' Then I let my smile disappear. 'Mark.'

Mark leant forward. 'Nice to meet you, Jess. Your brother seems to think we have a lot in common.'

'Like what?' I let my eyebrows rise and my glance swing over him. It had to be quick or I'd be swayed by the pressure of his square fingers. He had a serpent ring. Cool.

Before Mark could answer, I asked Tony where he worked. I gazed at him right through what he said back. I didn't dare check how Mark liked that! I can't remember now what Tony said he did.

The conversation developed over the pints and spritzers to the point where I'd forgotten I was supposed to be looking at Tony.

Nick said, 'She's a smart-arse, this one. Too clever by half. Got more GCSE's than I did. Going to take more than one A level, too.'

'School, such a fail,' I said. 'Who gives a—'. I took a slurp of my alcopop and kicked Nick's foot hard. I didn't want anyone thinking I was some nerd.

Mark was well taken with me, I could see. His eyes sort of gleamed and there was that half-smile set to his mouth. Nice lips. Extra, he looked at me each time he spoke, even if he was answering one of the others. It was good I'd put on ultra-lash mascara. It really makes the best of my eyes. They're my most attractive feature, though I've been told I have a lovely heart-shaped face. Compliments. I'm up for those.

I sort of joined in with the chat but I was already planning where we'd go, the Jazz Club or the Pink Clink, when Mark asked me out for Saturday week. Did I want any of my mates along or just me and him? *(Just me and himmmmmm, all of the time)*. 'Don't mind,' I said.

His arms were a very strokeable shape; soft hairs, firm muscles, who'd bet his legs would be the same. I do rate for a nice pair of legs. You can't feel the same about a man with great whopping thighs and blubber, but weak ones that don't fully straighten are the worst.

'Time to go,' said Tony at last, spoil sport that I guessed he was the minute I set eyes on him. Who said *he* was in charge of the wind down? 'I'll give you a hand, Mark.' He leant over and went to hoist Mark under his nearest arm.

Give him a hand?

'Let this lovely lady go first,' said Mark. 'Take her home, Nick. I don't want her seeing me struggle up or hearing the metal clanging on my false leg.'

'No, OK, Bro. We'll make a move first, then.' Nick jerked his head to me.

I didn't move, couldn't move at first. It was shock, horror. I'd dreaded weak skinny legs but skinny legs that are real are much better than a leg like iron that's – well – iron. I didn't look under the table out of decency. I'm not a rotten person at heart. But he was so lovely and I wanted him all to myself. But the whole of him, not three quarters. Metal leg! There'd be no Pink Clink or anywhere for dancing now. No clubbing at all, really, or we'd all have to stay sitting down. WTF was I going to say about Saturday?

'Come *on*, Sis! What are you still sitting for? Your glass really *is* empty and we're not buying another round. I've got things to do. Move yourself.' Nick was doing the big bro business and he went to the door.

I stood up, keeping my eyes on Tony's face. He wasn't so bad, really. Well, he'd be OK for someone else. 'Night, Tony.'

Then I held my hand out to Mark, a bit shakily. 'Bye then.'

He held it wonderfully softly, firm hands too. Shame, shame, shame. He was bare lush. He'd have been *sooo* right for me. If only.

'I suppose it is goodbye after all, then?' murmured Mark.

'Yeah, I reckon,' and I slid out of the bench to stand tall by my brother. Palming me off on his one-legged mate! Wait till I got him home.

I turned so that I didn't see Tony help Mark clank away.

It was raining outside and Nick didn't have enough for a taxi. A right flaming end to the evening, but I wasn't going to say anything.

'Well then,' said Nick, sounding like a clever clogs. 'Told you you'd like him. You were getting on like two chess pieces. Have I got good taste or not?'

I jabbed my elbow in his side. '*Not.*'

He sniggered and that was that. When we got in, wet through, I went and had a cup of tea with

Mum. Told her about my homework. That was how bad I felt.

I was as cross as a rained-off Saturday. Well, it was certainly a rained-off Saturday night. All that effort come to nothing.

And the following day we had relatives. Eek! So I had to stay at home for Sunday lunch.

Nick came in late after his rugby match.

'Did you win, then?' Auntie Em said, looking at his muddy state.

He grinned and nodded.

'And how's that handsome mate of yours, who broke his leg in the last match?'

Nick didn't look at me. 'Mark, you mean. Well, he says some girls won't look at him now that he's struggling with one leg in plaster. But there's plenty who will.'

Good job I'd finished eating or I'd have choked. I got up, pretending to help by taking dishes to the kitchen. I held the kitchen door hard across Nick's front and hoped his plateful of dinner would go cold. 'Scumbag. You wait when you have the hots for one of my mates. There'll be totally nothing doing. I'll turn them off!'

He was going weak with laughter. 'You should've seen your face, Sis.'

'Right, you derp! I'll tell the girls you have sick turns and throw up all the time. Mark's leg! You were all sending me up. I hate you.'

'Serves you right, Sis, for being so choosy.' He shrugged himself free of the door.

I watched his face. 'So – did he fancy me then?'

'What, with the way you treated him!'

'Yes, but did he?'

Nick started stripping off his filthy kit.

'God, you stink!'

'Healthy sweat. If you want an address so you can go up and draw your autograph on Mark's plaster, you'll have to make it up to me.'

I felt a tickling in my toes, or something. 'Like what?'

Nick grinned and wrote down an address holding it just out of my reach.

That's why I'm ironing shirts now. And it's *so* against my principles.

A FITTING MATTER

In 1999, bad Aunt Barbara, in her seventies, visited England once more. She just had to see the Millennium dawn in the country she was born in. She found me via a family history website. I never knew her sins but her name had been taboo all of my life so I met her with illicit excitement. I'd last seen her when I was two, she told me. Not since, thanks to the tensions between her and my parents.

Although my mother had often warned me against Americans during my teens, Aunt Barbara and I liked each other immediately. I liked her so much I invited her to stay.

'Better late than never,' she said with her American accentuation. 'I've always wanted to visit someone living in Kew village.'

She was active mentally and physically, very active, and at this moment was bending down to my laundry basket ready to hang out the next item on the washing line. 'Oho, the Veronica bra!' she said, waving it aloft. 'Fancy that!'

I smiled to myself. So it was known in the States too! The Veronica bra, I always buy that particular model. It's so perfect for my figure, it could have been made for me. I always wear a

Veronica and I always shall. I'll probably die in one (though I might undo it first).

It was my first bra, too, and carefully chosen. Aunt Barbara's commenting on it took me right back to that time when the Queen was young, the year of the Festival of Britain.

Mother was singing in the kitchen. That promised a good mood. She really wanted to go and probably Father had agreed to it.

I waltzed in and asked for some money to buy my first bra. Well, two, really, as I thought bras might have to go in the wash. I had two spare vests, after all.

My mother said I was too young for a bra. A school-girl didn't need one; her pectoral muscles were enough to support a bosom, given a good liberty bodice.

The shepherdesses on the mantle-piece wobbled as I slammed the door.

She followed me out into the hall. 'Slamming doors is not the answer. Whatever would your father say about that behaviour, madam, or the way you spoke to me? It's just not fitting for a well-brought-up girl.'

'Discussing a bra isn't fitting for a well-brought-up, middle-aged man.'

'Peggy!' she said. 'What has got into you?'

I told her what had got into me. 'A bust. I'm thirteen, *and* I have bosoms. All the girls in my set are going to be fitted for bras after school on Monday, and I want to go too. I need to, I've got more up top than some of them. My bosoms bounce about in hockey. It's embarrassing.'

She tutted and hm-hmmed and looked me up and down, then said I was too young to dress like a woman. 'I can't have you wearing a bra yet.'

'Why?' I screamed, 'I suppose *your* mother stopped you wearing a bra until you were married?'

She said, 'Your sarcastic tongue will get you into serious trouble one of these days, missy. You know we don't speak of my mother.' Her face had gone pink.

So I followed it up. '*Did* she stop you, then? Is that why we never see Grandmother or Aunt Barbara? Why there are no photos?'

She gritted her teeth and said we didn't have contact because we chose not. Father came in at that point and joined in. He only heard the bit about Grandmother. He said, 'We couldn't continue seeing her. It just wasn't fitting.'

'No, it wasn't,' Mother added primly. She always fell in with Father. It was because of being married to someone so much older than her.

When I'm adult, I'm definitely not going to do that. I opened my mouth to argue.

'Wait, Peggy!'

Mother saw I was set on pursuing the taboo subject of Grandmother's distant departure, if not bras, so she said she'd think over our discussion. She gave me one of her *staring hard* looks, pursing her lips and nodding her head. I knew this meant bras were not to be discussed in front of Father but that there was a glimmer of hope.

It took another three days of wheedling and opening up the subject of Grandmother, before Mother gave in over the bra. She clearly didn't want to, so she must have been desperate to avoid mention of her mother, particularly in front of Father. On the Monday morning she put money enough for three bras into my purse, then popped that into my satchel. 'Choose carefully, and nothing – *fancy* – now.'

'Fancy?' She may have meant sexy but she didn't say it. 'Fancy' was a word made for misinterpretation.

When I got into school, I looked round at my friends. None of the flat-chested girls were in our set. We lot grinned and nodded meaningfully at each other, which meant we'd all got our mothers to agree to our fitting.

We were extra noisy in afternoon school. We were excited. Getting our first bra!

The beauty of a school near Marble Arch meant we had Oxford Street at our doorstep for a whole hour before closing time. We went there nearly every school day. We'd planned to go to Selfridges and get fitted all together. That way we could share the embarrassment. Julia had told us that the lingerie assistant took you in a cubicle and put a tape measure around your bust. While you were naked! She said bras had to fit exactly right. There was cup size, uplift and support to think of, as well as how big around. Julia always knew these things.

I was glad that my absent and ill-regarded grandmother had paid all the fees for this school before she whisked off to Philadelphia, leaving scandalized relatives behind her for reasons which none of them would tell me. It took me away from the suburban school where I would have had to go, and put me in the company of sophisticated girls, or girls whose parents valued a sophisticated education — and sophisticated clothing. Even so, we had to dress in school uniform and behave with decorum, including wearing white lace gloves in summer. They soon got black, like our white collars. London was like that then, black grit on every flat surface. It was a mother's greatest anxiety, her daughter becoming soiled.

By three-forty, our French teacher said she was heartily glad to hear the bell for end of school. We had whispered, giggled and passed notes the entire lesson. When we got to the cloakroom, we took off our long socks and shoved them in our satchels and put on our stockings, nylon stockings. We'd all asked for them for Christmas presents. Only Julia was allowed to wear them at the weekends. For the rest of us it was allowed on special occasions only. Mother didn't even know I'd shoved mine in the back pocket of my satchel.

It was Julia who had the lipstick and passed it around. The others just dabbed it on anxiously. Julia had given herself a great cupid's bow. I tried to copy but mine was a bit smeary.

We had to sneak out of the side door so that none of the teachers would catch sight of our faces. Lipstick, nylons, that was for after the age of sixteen, or later still if we were nice girls.

Lingerie was on the second floor, well away from anything a man would want to buy. It all lay folded on the shelves and when you asked to see something, the assistant slid it out and whisked it into the air, then lay its silkiness on the counter. I'd seen Mother choose her petticoats like this. Each one had a different sort of lace on the top, and the most expensive petticoats had it on the hem too. 'So wonderful to have this in the shops again after the utility period,' the assistant told her.

There were white, pink and, sometimes, coffee-coloured petticoats, knickers and bras, but mostly it was all white. The cheapest bras were thick cotton and more like bandages. Luckily, none of the girls at my school needed to go for the cheapest.

We stood giggling before going up to the counter and asking for help. We whispered in between the racks of corsets, 'I don't want to be first,' and 'What size shall I ask for?' and 'Go on, you go,' 'No, you,' until Julia took charge.

'We'll all get measured and we'll all help each other choose.' She led the way to the counter.

The assistant seemed pleased to have a whole group to sell to, not annoyed at all. In the changing room, she took the measurements of each girl, while the rest of us politely turned our backs not to actually see our friends' bosoms and nipples. We exchanged news of our sizes delightedly, 'I'm 32A', 'I'm a B cup', 'I'm only 30', while Marcia was actually a 34C – huge – but then she did eat lots of chocolate spread at break-times.

We all tried on lots of different bras, peeping out from behind cubicle curtains with 'What about this one?', and 'Too baggy', 'Too lacy', and so on. It was more exciting than the coronation.

The assistant was really patient as we lined up with our purses and purchases. I chose three bras. I had only just enough money for them. The one I liked best was the Veronica with its silky V between my now beautifully shaped domes. 'Mastery' was cotton, and all right for every day. It had good uplift and the straps didn't cut in. I wouldn't have liked anyone to see it on me, but it was the one I was going to show Mother for approval, hoping she'd assume I'd bought three the same.

The girls made me buy 'Paris nights'. We all bought one, deep cut, lacy, really glamorous. 'For when we go to dances,' we said. Not that any of us had ever been asked to a dance yet, or even seen one.

I waltzed home wearing Mastery. I peeped in on Mother saying, 'I've got them,' and pulled up my vest to show her, letting the one bra serve for all three.

She looked, then bit her lip. 'It looks as if your straps are rather tight. Let them down.'

Upstairs in my bedroom, I lifted my vest and looked again. The straps were fine. Then I put on my red jumper that I hadn't worn for ages because of my soft lumps showing. So embarrassing. But now, with the circular stitching on 'Mastery' I had wonderful points instead of bumps.

At supper time there was smoked haddock with scrambled eggs, Father's favourite. But he sat in silence. He didn't even say, 'Marvellous, Victoria,' as Mother would have expected. He cleared the table with her, something he never normally did unless she had a headache. I got up to help but he told me to I'd better stay put.

I heard her mutter in the kitchen, 'It's the jumper, isn't it? Or what's under it? Reminds you of—'

'Time for bed, Peggy,' he called before stamping to his study.

It wasn't nearly time for bed. 'Why? Why, Father. *Why?*' I ran after him down the hall although I knew he wasn't going to answer before he clipped the door shut.

Then I came back to the kitchen, to wheedle Mother into explaining.

She said I had better not wear that bra with that jumper, it upset my father. He found it offensive, those points sticking out at him aggressively. I said I couldn't see what my uplift had to do with anyone else. I couldn't help it if I had a bust, unlike some people who were flat-chested. I didn't mean her. She wasn't flat, she was kind of bulky in that region, but she took it personally,

It wasn't the first time we clashed and it wasn't the last. My mother responded by telling me not to wear a jumper with a bra until I was older. I assumed she meant not in the house or with my relatives, those of them we still saw, which meant my father's folk.

I just had such stuffy parents. 'Why don't you just buy me a sandwich board and I'll wear that? Father can write on it *Flat Chests for Women.*'

He was just coming back to the fray and heard what I said. 'Enough, madam! We have 100 one hundred-per-cent more connection to female corsetry than I'd like, as it is.'

Mother nodded vigorously. 'Indeed yes.' Such a copycat, always apeing Father. I had no idea what they meant and thought they were extremely silly. I nearly said so, but I saw a coffee cake through the open crack of the larder door and thought better of it. It was my favourite.

During the next year, when I went out I wore bras like all my friends. We swapped notes and advice. As a result, I wore my roll neck jumper with Mastery, the circular stitching pushing my bust into points like a woman on a billboard; when I wore my summer dress with the boat neck, I wore Paris Nights, the lacy number. At all other times I wore my Veronica, even in front of my parents. It was just such a perfect fit.

I grew taller so my bust had less impact on them while they were gasping about my height. As I got older, though, I found Mastery too hard and Paris too soft. I was in a bigger cup size now. I tried other bras but I always ended up with the Veronica.

That was then, and I'm still wearing one now. It's the only bra that always fits beautifully.

'Ahem.' I came out of this reverie to find Aunt Barbara had finished all the hanging out of my clothes.

'Goodness, thank you so much, Aunt Barbara. Sorry I was miles away, or rather years. You noticed the Veronica? That's the bra I always wear. It's just such a good fit. I can't tell you what a hoo-ha it caused when I got my first bra.'

She took a little breath and her gleaming eyes showed she was excited. 'It would, dear, it would. Ladies corsetry, that's the business your grandmother worked in once we got to the States.'

'Oh?' I said, 'I never knew that! But – surely, working in corsetry wouldn't cause such a rift? We never even had a photograph of her, or you for that matter. Mother's mother and sister, very strange. Are you going to enlighten me?'

'I don't know that I should, dear. Your father would hate it, your mother too.'

'Aunt Barbara, I'm a woman of fifty-four, my parents have sadly passed away. I think you can feel free to speak now. It'll make your trip from the States worthwhile, especially for me.'

I could see she was caught between being desperate to divulge secrets and hesitant to go against my parents' wishes.'

'Come on. They'll never know, will they? I'll take you to the glass houses afterwards. Internationally famous. You'll want to tell everyone in Philadelphia about Kew Gardens. So come on, spill the beans.'

She didn't need that much persuading. 'I can't tell you how unhappy I was about the rift, but I was the younger sister, and didn't count. Victoria seemed to want our mother to stay a widow forever. It wasn't reasonable. Our father had been dead for three years before she got hitched again, and Eric was really nice. Victoria wouldn't even come to the wedding. The happy couple were going to the States afterwards. Eric was American so had to work there. Your grandmother took me with her when they went to Philadelphia because I was still only fifteen. Anyway I got on just fine with Eric. But Victoria wouldn't even give him a chance and she fell out with me because I was all for their marriage. Your parents were both appalled at it. Eric had been a traveller in ladies' underwear.'

'Oh how shocking!' I creased up laughing. 'Is that what Father meant by saying it "wasn't fitting" to know her? Surely not?'

'Not quite. Eric had become very successful by then and was opening a corset factory in Philadelphia. When they got over there, he made Mother an important designer for *YourBra. Inc.* She rose up the company quite rapidly. The Veronica was her most lucrative line.'

'No! The *Veronica, YourBra* was their company? That's amazing.'

'Yes. I was very proud of them both and we had a wonderful life-style. Your mother would have been over the moon if she had been there.

'So that should have made my parents happy to be in touch with them: success, money, life-style?'

'Sadly, no. We did hope. We came back to visit once. But it wasn't a success, except that we did manage to set eyes upon little you. There was too much bad feeling for more than the one visit.'

'About underwear, bras?' I giggled in a sad way. This bad feeling had separated me from important family. It was a bit of a puzzle.

Aunt Barbara shook her head, biting her lip.

'So what was the real problem?'

'Love. Your father had known your mother's father in his healthy days and when Pops died, was a great support to Mother. I remember him as a constant visitor during my early teens. He obviously hoped she'd turn to him for a second marriage, but it was Eric she turned to. In return, your father turned to my sister. Victoria, the oldest daughter, just turned seventeen.'

'Mother!' I could hardly speak. Eventually I breathed out, 'Father – so respectable, hoping to marry Grandmother and, disappointed, turning to her daughter! I always wondered why he was so much older than Mother.'

Aunt Barbara nodded, slowly. I had to sit down hard on my garden bench and breathe deeply. 'He acted much more scandalously than poor Grandmother, then. Who was he to say what was fitting!'

'Ah. Nothing more scandalous than behaviour like your own.' Aunt Barbara leant forward and tweaked the Veronica from the washing basket. She held it up like a flag. 'She always wanted to call you 'Veronica', you know.'

I had to laugh. 'Mother's hated middle name. It's just a perfect fit. It always has been.'

FINDING OUT

In late November the deadened skies inspired whispers that the village ghost was appearing again. Incomers who commuted from Tricklam to our county town spread the tale.

At that time, we were little more than kids: Jamie Denton and Sara Barrett, would-be journalist and photographer in our first year at the Uni's *Media Now!* course. Our first assignment threw us together, paired by the Uni management software.

Jamie was okay, I thought. Not a high flyer, but not a dead loss either. In our early assignments, we did all right in comparison with the others; 76 per cent; about rank three overall. Now some weeks into the course, we were all set an external task: to report a local story.

Our tutor, once a successful editor, now arthritic (paralytic according to rumour) assigned other pairs a variety of sensible leads but when it came to Jamie and me, we were given the most trivial of events.

Mr Bramlingham leant back into his chair as if he was still heading *The Times* or something. 'Right, you two. Find the Tricklam Trickster, or whatever causes this "ghost",' he barked at us, his untrimmed nasal hair bristling.

He prided himself on treating males and females equally, that is, harshly. He'd told me this when I applied for the course. 'Strict equality here, be certain of that, Miss Whatsit. No flouncing your shiny blonde locks and curly lashes at me. And you can leave your long words and A* English and Art behind you. Straight talk, quality of work and speed of delivery is all I care about. No fancy photo-art. Be on the scene, and back with your shots. That was my rule when I was editor of *Close-up Daily*. That's what I'm looking for now. Keep to the story and shoot it. No glamour on my course.'

He could afford to be objectionable because of the course's reputation and unbeatable results. Current high-profile journalists and media folk were graduates of this course and it was mega hard to get a place.

I couldn't help being blonde. I wanted to prove myself to the dinosaur and get his approval, but secretly I was finding this tough, go-get-it attitude very challenging. I'd worked hard on learning all I could about getting great shots, not minding what impossible acrobats this led me into. It never occurred myself to me to prepare myself for photographing ghosts, for pity's sake.

Even so, there was no way I was going to negotiate a change of set task and risk the wrath of the famous Bramlingham, even though the derision from our course mates was embarrassing. It must have been for Jamie too, but he didn't balk at the assignment either.

Perhaps one day, I could rely on Jamie, confide in him. He had a sensitive face, high, hard cheekbones, a rare but warm smile. I trusted him so far, but it was early days.

We set off obediently as the day ended, Tricklam bound, virgins in every sense.

'Tricklam! That dump,' Jamie grumbled, now we were out of earshot.

'Watch it,' I said. 'My mother reckons my ancestors came from there – though Dad's never admitted to it.'

'Trust us to get this rubbishy case, not the all-night comedy bash. That would have been so much fun.'

'We're not on the course for fun.' I knew I sounded up myself, but I wanted – needed – Jamie to be enthusiastic so I went on, 'This assignment'll challenge us. May be we should be glad to have it.'

Jamie looked at me with that 'Trust a blonde!' look. At least, that's what I assumed he was thinking.

Tricklam was only twelve miles away, a trickling village mainly along a B road that had been superseded by a bypass. It was a joke that Tricklam was well -named. Its reputation of producing incompetent drones wasn't helped by this ridiculous ghost story.

I drove – Jamie hadn't even got his licence yet, though that didn't stop him criticising my car-handling or me fancying him. He was quite tall and lean, with deep green eyes that seemed to look through the distance at something wonderful. One day perhaps he'd tell me all about it.

It was a dark grey night, and the village equally grey, the houses built in local stone and unadorned by flowers. They were homes that were practical at best, and the shabby curtains and unpainted doors sang out that they belonged to owners with no imagination. No motivation and no hope, perhaps. Unemployment was high around here.

At the only inn, the Stonemason's Arms, we took the publican's advice for the best beer, and adopted his cynical view of our assignment.

'Our ghost! You've certainly been landed with a dud article. Look, I'll pull you both a pint then you can hear the tale at first hand. I've only lived and worked here fifteen years, so what does a raw incomer know about it? There'll be plenty of "born here" locals coming in soon, ready to scare the socks off you for the price of a pint.'

And so it was. First a group of old men, whiskered and leathered, wagging their heads grimly and knowingly. Then two couples, sitting close together, sharing a bottle of wine. The male halves looked as if they might supervise work on the fields, except that no-one does that sort of things these days. The women were unfashionably dressed but in good wools that lasted. Each leaned against her man while talking in urgent alto tones. They made a symmetrical picture the four of them, the bottle of wine marking the centre like a tent pole. I stopped myself wondering what Jamie might write about this. I wanted a photo of these colourful locals, never mind the story.

We approached them slowly and overheard their words. It seemed that the ghost was a vibrant topic for locals.

'But it's not every night. She wasn't there Tuesday, that's for certain.'

'It's only when the clouds lie low.'

'There has to be a sort of mist. You wouldn't expect her in broad sunlight.'

I nudged Jamie. 'Go on – there's your start.'

Everyone always took to Jamie once he turned on his engaging smile. He'd surely get this lot talking.

He stepped forward. 'Excuse me. We're on a reporting assignment from the *Media Now!* course at Morley Uni. About this ghostly figure – can you help us?'

The foursome looked at each other, then the skinny woman said, 'It's an old tale and I heard it first from my Granny.'

The others nodded her on, 'Tell them, Jinny.'

'It doesn't happen every year, not by any means, but there's a woman. She appears at dusk—'

'Or after.' Her husband, a man with a big-veined nose, made sure she got her story right.

'Yes, down that muddy track near the new social housing, about a mile from here. You know there was once a large town the other side of it? All razed to the ground early in the eighteenth century—'

'—And never rebuilt, despite the plans.'

'Your hobby-horse again!' Jinny nudged her man.

'Yes. Useless council.'

'Nowadays there's just the kennels there. The track's more than a mile before that place and unlighted. It's way down it the figure's seen, by the little lake.'

'More like a big pond.'

'But the kiddies play there in hot weather.'

'Always did.'

Jinny and her husband stopped in synchrony.

Then the larger woman leant forward, her bulging eyes intent. Her voice was very low, almost a whisper. 'By the water she's seen. A long-haired woman, youngish, wringing her hands and looking desperate, her feet never moving, like they're turned to stone. And when she's approached, there's a cold wind comes. She looks entreatingly, and then she disappears before a person can reach her.'

As her whisper faded, Jamie asked, 'Have any of you ever seen her?'

They all shook their heads. 'But several folk have done recently, as they have in other years.'

'Let's be square with you. Someone saw her last night,' the second man spoke up. His beefy hands landed squarely on the table as if to emphasise the reality. 'There've been several sightings over the last three weeks. Our neighbour saw her, last night.'

'Yes,' his wife said slowly, 'she's an older lady, but very well thought-of round here. She teaches recorders at the school on Mondays. She was in quite a state, though quite definite about what had happened to her.'

Jamie was dithering. I said, 'We'd really like to know more.'

'Then you'd best go over to her place. Mary Phillips she's called. I don't want to tell it wrong.'

'Those old codgers over there,' said the man with beefy hands, 'they've all seen her over the years.'

'Don't we know.' His wife laughed. 'Everyone's been treated to their stories, bless 'em, but I shouldn't take them as gospel, if I were you.'

The others grinned and nodded.

Jamie said, 'Could we have the address of this Mary Phillips, please? Is she Miss or Mrs?'

'Oh always a Miss! Though she's a kindly old body.' Jinny drained her wine glass and held it towards her husband. We thanked the four of them and bought them another bottle of wine.

I brought my camera above the table level, but the women wouldn't agree to a photograph because they weren't dressed in their best. The beefy man asked to take one of me instead, without my coat on. Jamie whisked me away.

'They're not used to blonde bombshells in Tricklam,' he said.

I elbowed him in the ribs, 'Sexist.'

The old men, well into their night's drinking, were leaning against the high-back settles nearest the open fire. They were pleased to have an audience, even happier to be given an extra pint. I suppose our attention demonstrated to the rest of the pub clientele how important they were. Their stories were garbled and embellished by multiple tellings, enjoyable, nevertheless. I saw that Jamie was only writing down the minimum.

It was more important to get some atmospheric shots. This was quite easy. The roaring fire was nearby their table, old photos hanging under a beam behind the bearded elders. I captured them nodding at each other, a third wagging his stubby finger. It would look good on our project file, even if it didn't make the newspaper.

We'd done what we could so we left to visit this Mary Phillips. The walk to her cottage gave us a good idea of this village. There weren't many decent-sized houses and the roads we passed along had little to attract a house-hunter. The dingy houses were near enough identical, as if the curtains and paint had been bought in a bargain basement – a job lot, perhaps. They were the sort that showed in adverts for Before-and-After makeovers, in the Before category.

I looked them up and down. 'Perhaps it was true, Jake. This is a village of losers.'

'Snob. Mind what you say, especially if your ancestors lived here. Round the next corner we should find Mary Phillip's place.'

Round the corner, there were some older cottages with some character and style, backing on to open country. It was a surprise.

'Nice!' Jake pointed to one of them. 'That's her's.'

Our arrival was announced by her English bull terrier. Mary came out and placed a very firm hand on its collar while we explained. She was a sturdy lady with thickly shorn hair and heavy gold earrings, which perhaps she never took off.

I let Jake charm her into accepting our enquiries while I screwed up my eyes at the lady's hairline and nose, estimating the angle that might translate that chunky profile into something sinister. Or perhaps it was better that she looked totally sane and sensible, so that her (probably mad) story would be more credible.

She let me photograph her at her gate under my portable lamp. It was a good study of a village woman and dog, against a background of pretty cottage, stark trees and a slice of moon. Eerie enough.

Inside her small house, the bull terrier had its basket in view of the window. Mary certainly seemed a no-nonsense lady. In her sixties, retired from managing a small solicitor's firm, she made ends meet with teaching recorders and doing the accounts of local business men. She told her tale. Jamie was scribbling in his notebook.

Mary had been walking the dog the whole afternoon, for heavy rain was expected later. After returning home she found she'd lost her pocket watch somewhere en route. It was a good one her firm had given her, so she'd retraced her steps directly.

Dusk had fallen but she had a good torch with her. Just as she reached the lake, the torch flickered and went out. She was certain the battery was good, yet it wouldn't flick on again. The moon was thin and low. The dog suddenly whimpered and then Mary saw a figure just ahead of her. The woman was young with long wispy hair and a panicky expression. Mary called out, 'Hello. Anything wrong?' The woman didn't react.

Mary tried to go to her side but the dog wouldn't move, however hard she yanked his lead. She called out again, 'Are you all right?' Then a cold wind blew and without any sign of movement the woman just disappeared. The dog howled and Mary felt freaked. She hurried back up the track and soon the torch flickered and came on again. The dog pulled her home and she was very relieved to get indoors with all the lights on.

She hadn't gone to the lake since, despite the loss of her watch.

Jamie wasn't smiling but I could tell his spirits had revived, the way he was scribbling in his notebook at double speed. It was a gripping tale, more credible than the old men's version, which had included dragons flying from the woman's hair, transparent arms, smoke billowing from the whole surface of the lake as well as onlookers disappearing forever.

We thanked Mary and went back to the car to formulate a proper plan of action for the next day.

I almost expected the car not to start or some villager to come out and block our departure. 'Do you feel a bit freaked, Jamie?'

'Not yet. I think we have to come back and visit this pond or lake thing at night to get that. It'll be a waste of time but we have to do it.'

'Never mind. Mary's story will sound great when you write it up', I said. 'And my photos of her with the dog should be— ' I stopped. I didn't want to sound big-headed.

Jamie said, 'Mmm, but they'll expect pictures of the ghost herself. That'll challenge you!'

We laughed, raising our eyebrows at each other, knowing what we'd have to go through. We both stayed silent the rest of the drive home. The expected rain sheeted against the windscreen.

The following evening found us in Tricklam again. Instead of downing the good beer of the village inn, we ended up down a muddy track in the freezing fog.

There had been a sliver of moon but now it was covered by cloud. It was very cold. Our faces stung, although we'd put on several layers and wound scarves round our necks and over our chins. We'd both brought a torch as well as spare batteries.

'I'm not going to be caught out. It's not as if we've got a bull terrier to help us back home,' Jamie said. We trudged down the track towards the lake. No-one else was around. I was a bit scared already, turning my head in each direction. It was at such a time I valued being a pair not a solo photographer.

I nudged him. 'Look back now.'

The moon was scarcely detectable. Our torch lights spilled a thin stream in front of us, but behind us it was black. I rather wanted Jamie to hold my hand, but I just thought of Mr Bramlingham asking if I would prefer to stay at home and paint my nails, the old dinosaur.

We felt, rather than saw the lake at first. Our cheeks were damp with the mist which hung over its surface. I was dismayed there were no ghost-seekers for company, but I said, 'Good. There's no-one here to frighten the ghost away.'

We approached the lake and stood some distance from the edge, casting our torch beams all around. Nothing. We were quiet a few moments, waiting. Then I set up my equipment as silently as I could. I had no idea which direction I should have it facing, right side, left side or the far side of the lake? I told myself it was all for nothing, anyway. I'd just get some ghostly looking shots of bare-fingered trees, wisps of fog on the lake surface, that sort of thing. I might be able to sell some online. I decided I'd take a variety of shots, then call it a day. Jamie would surely be glad. How could he could jot down notes in the dark unless I held a torch? I kept these thoughts to myself. It would be stronger if it were Jamie who said 'Let's call it a day'.

My camera clicked into place on its tripod.

'Shhhh,' said Jamie, and nudged me hard in the ribs.

I looked round wildly. 'What? Where?' but before I could focus on any part of the swirling mists over the lake, a freezing blast of air seemed to suck me forward. I stretched out a hand for the tripod, for Jamie, anything, but nothing was there and before I knew it the lake lapped at my feet, the mist lifting, my hands empty.

Now I was not alone, a murmuring crowd was gathered beside and behind me. Where was Jamie? I opened my mouth to shout for him, but no sound seemed to come out.

A large man with a pole of wood lifted it to the water. A gasp went up and a jeer as two other men brought a young woman from I don't know where to the lakeside. She threshed from side to side, moaning.

I had thought it dark, but it was not so dark that I could escape the sight of the pitiful figure in a tattered gown, her hair floating in wisps round her tortured face. They lifted her under her arms, she screaming, begging, but the crowd bawled oaths at her and urged the three men on. They placed her on the stool, the large man balancing the other end of the pole. Another ran forward to help him while the others tied leather thongs around her writhing figure. Slowly she was lifted in the air and then lowered into the water and held there. The water must be near freezing point.

I yelled 'No-o-o-o' from a throat that was paralysed. Nothing sounded. I couldn't bear it, but I couldn't tear my gaze away.

A broad voice came from beside me. 'If she survives this, we'll know she's a witch, for sure.'

Several throaty cackles came from crones behind me. 'Not a chance she'll float.'

'But if she drowns?' I asked, my words disappearing like will'o the wisps.

The frantic woman rose into the air, sodden and gasping, her long hair streaming rivulets of water down her face and dress. 'My babies,' she shrieked. 'My babies! Alone in the cottage.'

But whatever she screamed next was lost to the water as she was submerged again.

I rushed forward and shouted, 'What on earth has she done to deserve this?' This time I heard my voice.

'She *fore-cast*, the witch. I lost all my chickens,' a woman nearby snarled.

'And I my cows, every darn one of them,' said the giant of a man.

Other voices murmured in the same vein.

'Forecast?' I was wringing my hands waiting to see any sight of hair or face on the surface of the water.

'Ye-ah,' the man said grimly. 'She *fore-cast*. Her own pig died and she fore-cast a great illness would come to all the animals of our village, and so it did.'

'Terrible large books she has in her cottage,' the woman said. 'Witchy books with foreign words. Spells that she put on our cattle an' swine, I don't doubt. Sure enough they died. Dreadful hardship it's brought, her fore-casting. Witch!'

There was another gasp as the young woman was brought once more to the surface, this time just a dripping bundle, green as the weeds twined in her hair and her gown. She looked inhuman. The crowd hummed. The air vibrated with their humming.

I ran forward. 'Pull her out. Please pull her out!'

One of the men threw her down on the bank and rubbed his hands on his leathery waistcoat. 'The work is done!'

The body lay unmoving like a slick of seaweed.

There was nothing I could do and my chest was heaving. I was heavy with guilt for not rescuing her. She was dead, no doubt about it.

I remembered her panicky screams. 'What about her babies?' I shouted round to the murmuring figures.

The men with the ducking stool cut her body from its thongs. More muttering, louder, and then the woman near me roughly shook my arm and spat,

'Witch's brood, Witch's brew,
Have nowt to do with 'em or
Evil for you.'

Would they kill her babies as well? Despite the heaviness in my feet, I fled from the lakeside, up the slope until I saw the spread of nearby cottages. Surely I'd hear crying if babies had been abandoned?

I was panting hard, partly from panic about the children, partly from a desperate fear to escape the darkness and scene of death. The babies may have had their mother torn from them by those men crashing into her home? I must rescue them and find some kind soul to take them in.

Most of the cottages were dark or with the merest glimmer of candle flame. I ran close to each, listening. It wasn't long before I heard heart-rending wails coming from a beaten-down place with a thatch little more than a bird's nest. I pushed open the door and the wails turned to whimpers as two tiny figures cowered together in the dark unheated place. I could see they were terrified of me.

Making pacifying noises, I looked around for something to wrap them in against the cold night. There was only rough paper for the baby who was wet to his armpits, and an old shawl for the little girl, hardly more than a baby herself although she was trying to be mother.

'Mammy, Mammy,' she was calling while she held onto the baby.

I couldn't take them to their mother, not then, not any time. I bundled them up, one under each arm. Perhaps because my own face was wet with tears, they didn't resist and fastened their eyes on each other.

At the nearest cottage, I banged on the door but no-one answered. At the next house I was waved fiercely away, and the next and the next. I ran through the field towards another cottage, smarter and sturdier than those before. A young girl came to the door, her hair half-braided, the brush still in her hand. She stared at my bundles, then at me.

'Are they the witch's children?'

'Please tell me a safe place for them.'

'Not here, for my father will return soon and he—' She stopped but I knew her meaning well enough. She looked down at the quivering bundles and her expression was soft. 'In the town there's a workhouse.' She pointed away, the opposite direction from the hamlet. 'Pretend you found them abandoned away in the fields. Point in a different direction and don't say from here, that's best. The workhouse'll take them in. They'll be cared for.'

I thanked her and ran the best part of the way to the town, for my attempts to wrap the mites was quite insufficient against the weather. It must have been over a mile, may be two, but the bundles seemed light. They were like dolls, too young for speech. I knew nothing of children, let alone babies, but I did my best to make calming noises as I clasped the damp bundles to my chest and ran.

At last I saw an ugly town with dirty alleys leading in and out of each other. Near the squat church was a wide- fronted building easily identified as the workhouse by the ragged figures around its doors.

I tried to calm myself and to look like a responsible person, not one who had witnessed terrible drama. The workhouse official was stern but not unfriendly. I think he saw that I was no needy mother in distress, but a well-wisher. The babes were quiet by then, perhaps smelling the aroma of vegetable soup which drifted from the open workhouse door.

I offered, 'I don't know who these babies belong to. I found them miles away from here, huddled near a shack, abandoned.'

To my huge relief, the two little ones were taken, kindly enough, to be warmly clothed, washed, fed and bedded down. They were so young they would forget their mother in a short time, poor little souls.

I pushed the heavy wooden door shut behind me. The ragged figures outside had gone. My gulps and tears were noisy now I was alone. I stooped to re-tie my shoelace and saw something glittering on the ground. I picked it up and poked it into my pocket.

There was no hurry, yet my way back seemed so much shorter. From the top of the slope, I peered down warily. To my relief, there was no sign of a body, no jeering crowd. As my shaky steps neared the now silent lake, a pale sun came up. Slowly it dispelled the mist and the dark waters shimmered.

It was then I came to my senses and wondered where Jamie was, and whether my camera equipment was still safely where I'd put it. Had I taken a photograph of anything that had happened? Was there any record at all?

From some distance I could see the tripod where I had left it, the bag of equipment beside it. Thank God! There were many hundreds of pounds invested in that college equipment. Imagine Mr Bramlingham's face if I'd gone back without it! But there was no sign of Jamie. The lake was deserted, too muddy around its edges for comfortable walking and still cold, although the sun was in the sky by now. I checked my equipment. All was well, so I packed it up and scanned the area for Jamie. Nothing.

He must have made off without me. Great! He'd called it a day unilaterally. No thought for my safety, obviously. Equality? I'd been treated just the same as another guy, perhaps worse. He'd probably gone to the inn where we had recorded the first stories, was it last night or the night before? I felt confused and unsure what I had seen or where I had been and for how long.

I set off for my car. When I reached the inn there was still no sign of Jamie nor of anyone. Silence. The landlord must still be sleeping so I didn't try the door. I was tired myself, dog tired.

Without even considering alternatives, I drove off and made for my flat and my bed. At home, I made tea and drank two cups then showered in very hot water. I wasn't hungry. The bed looked the safest place on earth. I lay down, not thinking, not daring to think. I didn't want to clarify what I remembered.

Before I knew it, it was daytime. I woke in a panic, sensing I should be at Uni, should have been at Uni. Sure enough the phone was blinking, full with answer-phone messages.

One was from Jamie, sounding very sober. 'Sara? It's Jamie – are you there? Er – did you get back last night . . . ? I didn't get into uni today. Can you come over – or meet me somewhere?'

Jamie. He'd left me at the lake, hadn't he? Or had he been with me the whole time last night? I investigated my memory painfully. I could see him standing by me as I set up the tripod, but not later. Swallowing a dreadful nausea, I made myself re-visualise the ducking, the crowd. I couldn't get Jamie into that picture. He hadn't been there, not that I could recall. Not when the green-entwined body lay beyond hope on the bank. Nor on my run to find the babies. And he certainly hadn't been at the workhouse.

Did he take off before it all happened? In fact, how did he get home? Had he been there at all after I set up my camera? If not, would he believe what I told him? I couldn't remember photographing anything, nor even having my gear around when the ducking began. I imagined my conversation with Mr Bramlingham and my cheeks grew hot. And what could Jamie write if he'd seen nothing? In fact, what the hell were we going to produce for that feature? It would be best if we faced the boss together, united. But how could I convince Jamie of what I'd experienced?

I rang him, non-committal. 'Hi Jamie. I didn't go into Uni today either, stayed in bed. I didn't see you last night after we got to the lake. Are you ok? How did you get home?'

'Hitched when I found you'd gone without me.'

'Gone without you?' Then I made my voice go normal. 'I saw *you'd* gone. Fine gentleman and protector, you are!'

There was a sort of snort. I swallowed my resentment. After all, he was a year younger than me. I just said, 'Look, you'd better come round. We need to discuss the assignment.'

When Jamie arrived, he looked dreadful, grey and drawn. He looked — like a man who'd witnessed what I had witnessed. He stared at me for some moments.

He said, 'You all right? You look ill.'

'I slept for ages. You?'

'Slept badly. What happened? Where were you?'

'By the lake, watching.' I was wary. 'What did you see?'

'You saw something then?' Jamie was being wary too.

'Yes. Go on, you're the feature writer. Describe it. Let's swap.'

60

'It sounds crazy, Sara, but if you saw something too I won't feel such a prat.'

'No, you're not a prat. Go on.'

Jamie looked at the floor. 'At first I thought it was just a wisp of fog. I told you, but you didn't answer. I went forward. I thought it was on the surface of the lake but then it was like clothed in a gown which flowed to the ground, green, weedy sort of. So it must have been standing at the lake's edge. Then a face grew out of the mist – grey-white, green almost, haunted-looking, a begging expression. Did you see her?'

'Yes. I saw her.' I swallowed. 'Did you see anyone with her?'

'No. She was alone. Looking at me as if I was the only human on the planet. I could see she was desperate and I wanted to ask her what I could do, but my throat closed up. I couldn't speak. I heard shrieking – but it didn't seem to come from her. It was distant, ghostly. She went on staring at me while I was rooted to the spot. Then she disappeared, like she was sinking into the lake. Did you see it all? Tell me I'm not brain-damaged.'

I drew breath. I hadn't expected this. 'I saw her, but it was different. Worse. She was real; alive at first, then drowned. Men brought her to the lake. They tied her on to a stool, ducked her in, a crowd shouting all around. I *wanted* to save her.'

I'd have to tell Jamie the rest. 'Where were you? It was as if I was there alone all the time.'

'I was there, by the lake. No-one around at all. I was alone with her. After she disappeared, I sort of came to. I was on the far side; I can't remember us walking there.'

'We didn't.'

'It was spooky and so cold. I ran back to where we'd stood at first. I looked around for you, for the tripod and gear but you – it had all gone. I guessed you'd panicked or something and run off. But without anyone there, I wasn't sure whether I was imagining everything, dreaming it up because I'd so wanted to write a good feature. I ran back to the inn where we'd left the car. No car, and when the landlord hadn't seen you—'

'He was open at that hour?'

Jamie stopped short with a gasp. 'Wow – I didn't think. Yes. It was morning by then. Where had the hours gone? When I got to the pub the landlord was swilling out. He helped me hitch a lift. How could it have been morning – we only set up your gear when it first got dark? When I saw the – whatever it was – and came to, I had to make my way back to the inn by torchlight. Did you come back in the dark?'

'No,' I said, unnerved. 'First light. After I'd done everything, run miles.'

'Run miles?'

'I'll tell you in a moment. But a lot happened. A hell of a lot. But you were there all night, longer than me.'

'My God! But as soon as I got back I left a message on your answer phone and—'

'— and I got it the next day. I lost a whole day.'

Then I told Jamie all I had seen, the body, the nightmare of it. He was pale already but my story didn't help. We went over and over it, checking, checking – our own memories as much as anything. I'd had the worst of it, we agreed on that.

At last, we each had to accept the story of the other. We couldn't discount any of it.

At the same moment we both turned to the camera, lying on my desk. I picked it up. I was sure I hadn't been holding it at the time of the ducking. But would I have caught anything in the shots I'd taken before there were any apparitions?

We went through the whole lot. No. There were some eerie shots of the lake, that was all. You could see it was deserted, dark, and I had picked out a few trees in the background, spooky enough with their bare, spiky arms. There was a suggestion of wispy cloud near the surface of the lake but nothing anyone could possibly interpret as a figure, not with the wildest stretch of the imagination.

'What the hell am I going to write?' Jamie groaned. 'It all comes down onto me, now. We can't even back each other's stories properly. We saw her – what do you reckon – at different times? You when it was happening, and me afterwards, after she was a ghost? Or before? Before the crowd came? But she rose from the lake. If I write it as you saw it, there are no witnesses, no photos, no evidence but your account. Bramlingham will have me on toast.'

'And have me toasted too, for "a pitiful effort". I can hear him saying it. Bellowing it, more like. *These blurs supposed to be your shots of the scene? Try cleaning your lens!'* I put my head in my hands.

'And if I write what *I* saw, he'll say I'm just pretending I've seen what the villagers have been muttering about all these years. Like those old lags.'

'Hey, Jamie! At least you've got Mary Phillips' story, and I've got her picture with that dog. Local interest. It's something. We could both just stick to that.'

'And miss out the whole drama, a real story? With all the rest of our course-mates turning in an ultra-professional assignment? No, let's go for it. We'll just have to back each other up.'

A touch encouraged, we decided to turn up at Uni and seek out Mr Bramlingham jointly, to brave it out.

The third years' session was in full swing as we slunk into the media unit. They looked at us, first years, the dregs, the fall guys, the mats for wiping their boots.

'We need to see Mr Bramlingham.'

We were propelled – firm hands behind our lean shoulders – towards the half-glassed door which was normally only approached with specific instruction, and then very nervously. We had to withstand the roar as Mr Bramlingham saw us. 'You two. At last! No notification. Two full days missed – of the first year major assignment of all things.'

We both spluttered out our *Sorrys* and *We can explains*.

'Oh yes! Too hard was it? A village down the road. Why not transfer to something that suits you better? Cat management? Flower arranging?'

It was difficult not to just turn and run. We'd already decided to take it in turns to report what we'd seen. As we gave the gist of it all, Mr Bramlingham snorted and scowled, his eyebrows worming up and down, but we pressed on.

'Yeah, yeah, hallelujah. Witnesses?' Mr Bramlingham bawled in typical style. 'Shots?'

We produced what we had. He bellowed the expected at us.

'And you were intending to write up this crap as a feature?' he spat at Jamie. 'Some ghost witnessed by the local drunks and a Sunday school teacher! You expect me to believe this – let alone mark it! Come on, admit it! You took the villagers' stories, then took off for a night and day on the town. Paired off, did you?'

Jamie, red-faced, shook his head, stood his ground. 'Pairing off' was probably the worst of the outburst for him.

I showed the photos we had, without saying anything, while Jamie told his tale in full.

Then it was my turn. I didn't look at Mr Bramlingham. My neck was dripping sweat, given that mine was far the more incredible account. Somehow I gave it. His eyebrows were almost covering his eyes as I got to the leaving of the babies at the workhouse.

'A very creative touch! Are you serious, girl? You expect me to show the course evaluator this crap? A ghost seen by a half-baked first- year student hardly out of short trousers, and a medieval ducking witnessed by his blonde cookie! I'd never live it down.'

Now fury overlaid my fear. I was going to face this out and tell Bramlingham he was out of order. The sweat was trickling down to my back. I put my hand in my pocket for a tissue to dab my neck. As I pulled it out, something fell to the floor. A gold watch. We all stared at it. This object spoke for itself.

'What the devil's that?' asked Mr Bramlingham.

I picked it up slowly, remembering how I got it. My heart thumped hard. Perhaps now he'd have to consider my 'facts'.

'I picked this up outside the workhouse, after I'd left the babies,' I said.

Jamie's face swung swiftly to mine, alive with both shock and elation. 'You didn't tell me that. Mary Phillips lost her watch!' He turned to the desk. 'The woman we inter-viewed, the photo with her and her dog, she lost a watch the afternoon she saw the ghost – somewhere on a long walk with the dog. That's why she went back to the lake in the dark – she went everywhere she'd walked to find it.'

Mr Bramlingham looked so hard at me I thought I'd disintegrate. Did he think I'd stolen it off her? He held out a large hairy hand for the watch. 'Phone number? Woman's name again?'

We supplied these and stood breathless while he held the telephone conversation in the social tones he reserved for people who weren't students on his course. He put the receiver down very carefully, his eyebrows almost covering his beady eyes. 'She's coming in to collect it. Barrett, we'll need some more shots.'

'Right.' I held my breath.

'What are you waiting for?' he bellowed to Jamie. 'Get the hell out of here and get your fingers on the keyboard. There's a great story to sell. I don't give a hang whether you've both exaggerated or even concocted this, but it's going to sound good. If you end up with your necks on the rack I can rid myself of the pair of you. Or maybe I won't. It's a story, it's topical, it's local. And it's not every day this course gets a corker. We could get a dollop of extra funding next year if this goes right.'

Jamie disappeared before Bramlingham's sentence was finished.

'And you, madam photographer. Leave washing your hair tonight. Go to county archives and ask for the old parish maps. I want to know *exactly* where that workhouse was. Exactly, mind. To the millimetre. Photograph the detail.'

If we had been virgin journos before, by the time our story had run its course we certainly were not. We had ghost-hunters, parapsych-ologists, historians, sensation-seekers haunting the Uni campus. They wanted to interview and photograph us, even put us on television.

I hassled the county record office until it was found that the old workhouse stood exactly where the kennels are now, the kennels where Mary Phillips always had to bend down to put a lead on her dog. When I went back to see her she said the dog was always wild to get into the kennels. So she always used that point to put him back on the lead. She must have dropped the watch as she bent down, she reckoned.

How could that have been, the miles I ran from the lake? That was only one of the mysteries that wasn't answered.

The Stonemasons' Arms made a mint that season thanks to the drama in its village. We had drinks on the house whenever we cared to visit – which was only when we absolutely had to. There was always a crowd around us, we couldn't relax. No-one seemed to realize that it wasn't fun for us. We were both totally freaked out, we didn't have to act for the television programmes. Even now, I hate ponds and little lakes and never go near them in the dark. It's the same for Jamie. The experience cemented our friendship. I needed his support, never mind equality of the sexes.

A keen local historian loved my story. He found an account of a ducking at that lake for "witchery". It was hundreds of years ago, too long past to identify names. That town burned down to nothing just afterwards and was never rebuilt.

I asked him to research the workhouse records. They had remained in the parish chest in the church until the eighties. He promised to trawl through them.

Jamie came with me when I visited the historian again, some weeks later. 'Might be a story in it, I suppose,' he said.

The historian brought us in to his dusty study where documents were spread all over the table. He looked at me, then more deeply into my eyes, as if I might disappear. 'Workhouse Records. Such a very strange coincidence,' he said. 'There is only one pair of little children who were brought at night by a stranger. They're recorded as Sara and James Denton.'

'That's my name!' said Jamie.

I sat down hard, and Jamie drew his breath through his teeth so sharply that it whistled. Then he leant over the table to see the handwritten entry. 'It's true, Sara,' he said. 'The names are quite clear. So my origins are here. And didn't you say your dad came from that village?'

It was that night I took Jamie home for the first time. History suggested we belonged together.

'The babies may have been brother and sister, but we're not.' Jamie stayed the night. Well much longer than a night, in fact.

He wrote up another good story for the paper. It pleased the boss who was already looking at us with a bit less derision. Other students, third years, told us he dined out on the story quite a bit. We were certainly brought in to his office to be displayed to his media friends, right up until we graduated, and after.

It did Jamie's reputation a great deal of good at an early stage in his career. But I left journalism, worked for a local studio and concentrated on child portrait studies, weddings and graduations. It felt safer, somehow.

'One of us should keep more regular hours,' said Jamie, as he served out my beef casserole in our new kitchen.

I ate it all up contentedly. It's good to find out who you are.

STAYING PUT

I remember that icy moment which you forget, which you say never happened.

My left cheek stung from your slap, the only warmth on that freezing day. You lunged for the car when I tried to drive away, and cracked the wing mirror.

At that moment Father Worthy's reflection, segmented like a stained glass window, appeared in it and I thought he was coming to save me. But he waved to you. He picked his way carefully, to not to slip on the icy road, looking down at his shiny toe caps while his robe swept the snow and gathered a frosty hem, a broderie anglaise fit for a priest.

(Yes you *do* remember Father Worthy, who called to intervene when the matter of babies came between us. *You* called on him, not me. I sat there, the two of you patronising me, both of you saying you knew exactly how I felt. You and your uterus imagined between you; your shared understanding of my mind and emotions, as well as my body. Wonderful men!)

In one jagged fragment of wing mirror I saw Father Worthy turn towards a house where the curtains blew free even on a day like that day. In the drive, children's garden toys lay neatly like workmen's tools. His robe lifted like a wave, up one side, down the other, as he stepped over the toy tractors and scooters on his way to their front door.

I imagined the next half hour. How he would glow and pat the heads of the planned and desired little ones. How he would nod in satisfaction as he advised their parents and listened to their agreements. And then they would pray. What for, now? Not for me, trapped in a car, trying to retreat.

You thrust your full weight on the bonnet, dug your heels in, glared through the windscreen, daring me to drive off. 'Listen. You're mine forever. Right? You don't have a choice.'

(*I heard it*. You *know* you never said it, that you never heard me speak.)

In the snowy air my silent thoughts screamed, *I want to go.*

Who knows what I said, what you said? I only know that the car stayed still, not scuttling off across the ice, not zooming to freedom. I believed your power was enough to overcome the engine, brake, accelerator, clutch, suspension, and me. I flinched away from you, my eyes on the mirror.

Father Worthy reached their front door, lifting one long leg to step over a tricycle. With shock, I saw that under that robe there were dark trousers, just like yours, just like any man's.

I looked back and saw your hands, maroon and mauve with cold. Senselessly, I reached for your gloves as if, as long as your hands were protected against the frost of that day, I could press my foot down and move your bulk from the bonnet and my warmth from you forever.

But the car remained, the snow a sludge around its tyres, for I stayed sitting, my foot paralysed, a sliver of ice in my heart. Forever yours.

EATEN UP

Prunella's mother had foresight. Decades before the benefit of fish to the brain and 5-a-day fruit and vegetables was commonly known, she advocated eating them.

Here she is back in that time: switching off *Postman Pat* so that Prunella can concentrate on eating her tea.

The tot watches as the grey blob grows smaller and paler until it disappears from the middle of the television screen, her lips pressed shut. Her mother holds a fork dangerously close to Prunella's mouth.

'If you don't eat those sardines up you won't grow up to have babies.'

'Don't like sardines.'

Prunella is not a good eater-up. She often has this conversation with her mother. Other days it's:

'You've left all that lettuce and half your meat. All that goodness. You won't have anything inside you for making babies when you're grown up.'

'I like the chips. I like the ketchup.'

'Chips! Ketchup! There's nothing good in them. Nothing worth having. You can't make good babies out of chips and ketchup.'

'I don't like meat and I don't like the lettuce.'

'Then you don't like babies.'

'I do. I like babies.'

'Then eat up, and perhaps you'll have some one day.'

'I can't. I can't.'

Pru's mother lifts herself up from the dining chair, bosom first. She's been sitting on it for forty minutes. No -one can say she didn't try. 'Then don't eat it. Get off with you. I give up. I've tried to warn you. It's your own fault, Prunella.'

Prunella runs into the garden to play with her plump dolly. She sticks thorns into its rubbery stomach in the hope it will deflate.

The arrival of one brother then another has its advantages although that doesn't deflect their mother from her primary purpose.

'Let's see you eat up like your brothers, Prunella. Another mouthful, come on.'

Pru secretly donates many mouthfuls to boys who have no problem eating for three.

Despite her disinterest in eating, Prunella grew up and even out a bit. She began to brush her hair twenty times, one fifth of her mother's pronounced essential, and learned to describe its brownness as 'chestnut'. College and then work meant she got to meet men, who found her leanness elegant. Some she went out with and let them call her Pru. One of them asked her to marry him. She wanted to, but felt she should be honest, fair.

'I'd like to, Andrew, but perhaps you shouldn't marry me.'

'Why on earth not?' He stood sturdily in a feet-apart stance, demonstrating grounded-ness. 'I love you.'

'I don't think I can have babies.'

'Then we won't have any. Anyway, why do you think you can't?'

'I don't eat very well. I've never eaten well.'

'Well I have. I do. And it's the men who make good strong babies. If we want them. And perhaps we don't.'

Can't have babies? Of course Andrew had to meet such a challenge as soon as possible, and he did. He had Pru pregnant before she'd even chosen a wedding ring, or the negligee for her honeymoon – and well before she'd told her family the news.

He strode round wearing a smirk like a bloke at an interview whose uncle is the boss.

Pru, of course, wouldn't believe the evidence. 'I can't be. It's just nerves. Excitement about marrying. I don't think I can have babies.'

'Well I can obviously make them and you're having mine. That test kit's just proved it.'

'I just don't feel I am. I can't be. I'd know. I feel really well.'

'You are well. Blossoming. Having babies is going to suit you. You'll see.'

Pru thought she had better speak to her family quickly. She put on a sweeping African print poncho over cargo pants. Her brothers grinned and raised their eyebrows. One sent her a text from the kitchen. *Bringing parents into 21st c?*'

'You look well, Prunella,' her father greeted her, a question of hope on his brow.

She blushed and smiled, looking down and away from her mother who was probably gathering her thoughts about the cargo pants. 'I'm going to get married. His name's Andrew. We thought we'd do it quite soon. We don't want a big affair.'

Her father was quick to respond. 'So you're in love, Prunella! It suits you.'

'About time, Prunella,' said her mother, 'though I'm surprised you haven't brought Andrew to meet us first. There isn't anything wrong with him, is there?'

Pru's brothers suggested a few things that might be.

When she'd swatted her brothers, Pru put her parents' antiquated minds at rest. She told them how Andrew was a marketing manager at an important firm in their town. She told them that he hadn't been married before nor taken drugs nor been to prison even to visit a friend. He didn't have a drinking habit. He lived with two other men in a flat but wasn't gay. They had met at Angela's party six months ago. Pru hadn't chosen a wedding ring yet, but she was going to, probably Saturday.

Her parents seemed really glad to think of Prunella married even though it meant she would be leaving home. She was twenty-four so she hadn't been rash and stupid.

Andrew arranged the wedding and suggested a venue for the reception. Prunella's parents paid and all the guests who mattered decided to come. Prunella bought an ice-blue dress which fell from a satin band below her bust. It looked delicate and flowing at that moment.

The size of Pru's stomach eventually led her to accept that she was pregnant. She went to ante-natal classes and met other pregnant people. The idea of having a baby started to become real. She wondered what the baby would be like, given that she had never been one to eat up. It might be very skinny.

'It'll have my genes,' said Andrew confidently.

'I hope I can get married before it comes,' Pru worried. 'It would be nice to be married first.'

Pru didn't have to tell her parents and friends. Size did it all. She was glad she didn't have to drop any hints to her mother, who eventually gave in to the evidence of her eyes.

'You look larger – you look *pregnant*, Prunella!'

'I am.'

Her mother sat down in a heavy, defeated way, one hand on her ample bosom. 'Well! It's a miracle you can have any babies, the way you ate all your life or rather, didn't eat. You're a dark horse. What date?'

They told her.

'It would be nice if you could get married first! Now I suppose you'll say I'm out-of-date. It's certainly a surprise for me.'

'Delighted, Pru,' said her father. 'It's as well to get on with having a family while you're young.'

Pru nodded.

Her mother gazed hard at her, as if Pru might transmogrify. 'Does the doctor say you're all right?' she asked disbelievingly. 'He does? Must be all right then. Amazing. Now I'll come with you to choose the baby clothes. Get white, then the sex doesn't matter.'

Pru already knew she was having a boy but it would be nice for her mother to have something else as a surprise. She'd already given her one when she moved into the fourth- floor flat Andrew had rented.

'We deserve a bit of time to ourselves before we're joined by a third person,' he said.

Now convinced a baby really was coming her way, Pru quickly read some baby-care books. She talked to friends who were mothers already. They would know what to do.

The baby was in a hurry so came before the wedding after all, but not before the baby clothes were hanging in the baby cupboard, and the Moses basket and the changing mat and bag of baby goods were on the floor of the spare room. Pru came home with her ten-day- old baby who was rather premature, but healthy and quiet. He was called Malcolm.

Andrew was proud, totally confirmed in his predictions. Pru was happy. She hadn't eaten up and had still grown up to have babies. Well, one baby, and he wasn't skinny. Furthermore, Pru found she liked babies despite the work.

The wedding was smooth running. Pru and Andrew were able to enjoy it because instead of being nervous about a Big Day or about The Future, the future had begun already. They were having a party, a wedding party and a day off from baby care. Everyone made a fuss of them. The food was good. Pru's dress flowed more fully than it would have done a month before. She glowed. Andrew loved her. The baby, lying quietly with an elderly relative, awaited the return of Pru's attention.

Malcolm was an easy baby but he appeared to crave company. Before Pru had quite got used to having him around or to being a mother or even to accepting that she could have babies after all, she got pregnant again. Of course she didn't believe it, but Andrew did.

'You're bloody pregnant again! Good God! All that crap about "can't have babies"!'

Pru could see that he was really pleased at the idea. It was as if he'd been promoted or awarded an 'A' grade at baby-making. 'It's not certain, Andy. Perhaps I just haven't got back to normal after Malcolm. I'll probably come on next month. Sure to.'

She didn't. She didn't the next month either, so once more she had to accept that Andrew was right. Lucky she hadn't given away any of Malcolm's first- size baby clothes!

Pru organised another drawer. She re-lined the Moses basket. Malcolm lay and watched her from his cot.

'You'll soon have a play-mate, my baby,' Pru smiled at him. She arranged her ante-natal classes.

'It's very soon after Malcolm,' she said to Andrew. 'It's surprising, really. Usually people have two years or more between their children. They'll only be thirteen months apart. And that's if the next one doesn't come early like Malcolm.'

'Doesn't surprise me. Remember I told you about my cousin who has the large family?'

'No! You didn't say.'

'Perhaps I didn't. At the time, having babies or not was rather a sensitive subject in your family, remember.'

'Now it isn't, is it, so tell me more.'

'Cora was at the wedding, the one with the bolshie husband.'

'What did she wear?'

'Something dark. Purple I think. Threw her arms around a lot when she danced. Three of their kids are triplets. They didn't bring them.'

'Triplets! Three at once! All that feeding! You'd really have to love babies. Amazing, to have triplets in the family.'

'Genes. Told you not to fuss when you thought you couldn't have any, didn't I?'

'You could have said about triplets. Did you visit when they were babies?'

'Great fun! Lots of babies, lots of toys, lots of noise. I didn't go often.'

Pru decided to fully concentrate on her pregnancy. It had all been too new, too unexpected, last time. And it had clashed with the wedding and moving out of home. Pru looked at Malcolm and tried to remember him a month ago, two months ago, four months ago, to gain a sense of how small the new baby would be. She couldn't remember back. Right now, Malcolm was her baby. She cuddled him, and he seemed quite small enough.

He was still being admired in his pram when Pru went into labour. Natalie returned home to be the play-mate and source of frustration to Malcolm for the next sixteen years. Her full face and dimples invited devotion and thus she enjoyed a full year of her mother's attention before Pru began her strange feelings.

After several repetitions of these words, Andrew asked her what these feelings were exactly.

'I feel kind of bloated,' she said. 'As though I've eaten loads and loads of bread. But I've eaten hardly any.'

'Not pregnant again? Certainly hope not! Really. We'd have to move – although the four floors with the buggy is good exercise for you.'

Pru looked at him hopefully. 'You did say the stairs were tiring after your long day at work. And the babies will need separate rooms when they're not babies any longer.'

'Mm. Perhaps you're not pregnant. Getting rather expensive now. Especially if you're going to start Malcolm at that nursery group. Two's enough probably. One boy, one girl. Perfect. Both of us happy.'

'Yes. No, I'm not pregnant. Not quite recovered after two babies, probably. I think it may be Caringa or Cloatia or some word like that. That's bloating in your gut, or too much bread fermenting, I think. I read about it somewhere. I'll go to the doctor.'

She did. The doctor told her she was pregnant. He felt her stomach. 'Twelve weeks probably, even if you have had periods.'

'Three months! My baby's not long had her first birthday.'

'Indeed. Then this one's a big baby. Twelve weeks is my estimate. But you'll get your hospital appointment through in a while. Meanwhile, step up the iron. Here's a prescription. Make sure you get enough rest.'

Pru went away and had a coffee in a white hotel lounge while her parents were still baby-sitting. She felt rather stunned as she returned to climb the stairs. A house with carpet and banisters would be nice.

This time Andrew sighed. He said he was pleased, but after this one they must leave it at that. 'Or we'll have no life at all. Nothing but bath-times, tidying toys and visiting theme parks. Three's enough, isn't it.' It wasn't a question. Pru agreed. She loved babies, but three was quite enough.

At the hospital appointment, Pru learned that three was not going to be the total size of their family. The specialist couldn't say how many yet, but thought there were more than two babies.

'More than two! But I've got two babies already. One's two and one's one.'

'And now there'll be four children, or more. It's a shock, isn't it?' the specialist sympathised. 'But you've got several months to adjust to the idea. Alert your relatives and friends now. You'll need all the help you can get. Plan ahead.'

Pru staggered home. She had been feeling really bloated all this time and Malcolm seemed suddenly heavy when she lifted him out of the bath. Natalie lay in her cot with a knowing expression. Then she filled her nappy noisily and with visible satisfaction.

That night Pru had to break the news to Andrew, to everyone. Andrew went to the pub and came home very late.

Otherwise there was a lot of excitement. All that Pru could think of was that she only had one Moses basket, one set of clothes.

She contacted Andrew's cousin to ask advice. Cora was sympathetic. Her triplets, two girls and one boy, were now nine years old and life was manageable. (Only now?) Cora said she was dependent upon school days for her sanity and well-being. 'But you'll manage. You find that you do manage, even though it seems overwhelming and chaotic at the time.'

'But you didn't have two babies already,' Pru wailed. 'Your others were quite big when your triplets came. How will I manage?'

'Shame Chatham's such a long way away from Chepstow or I could help. Try to get Andrew's parents and yours to step in.'

Pru sat in the little bedroom that housed Malcolm's truckle bed and Natalie's cot. Natalie crawled around both and looked at her mother, dimples working. Pru wondered how Natalie would get any attention. Malcolm would at least have nursery group. If they could afford it.

Both sets of parents provided extra baby clothes, extra equipment. Andrew talked about the coming event at work before the annual promotions. A sympathy vote was better than no vote.

A senior manager in the know got Andrew an interview with a newspaper. The outcome was a sponsoring by Chuckles, a baby toy firm. Chuckles said that in the event of triplets, for the babies' first two years they would provide everything in return for regular photos, features in their Chuckles magazine and advertising in all their sales outlets.

'It won't be that bad, being on adverts, will it?' Andrew put it to Pru, 'And it will solve our financial problems for a while. God knows what we'll do after the two years are up!'

'I don't think I can manage it all alone,' said Pru, weepily. 'Can't you get extra paternity leave?'

There was no immediate answer. Andrew had been thinking of the opposite – working harder and longer, and of being away from home for a greater number of hours. There were four retired parents to help Pru, after all. They'd step up.

He spoke hopefully. 'Perhaps the specialist is wrong. It may only be twins. Then you'll manage. Natalie's easy enough. Your mother will help. Mine have offered. They even said they'll move to live nearer.'

The specialist wasn't wrong. Pru gave birth copiously. It was more than two babies. It was more than three, in the end. Quads. All boys.

'They're not identical, any of them,' she breathed to Andrew when he dared enter the labour ward.

He was utterly wordless but gave her a kiss.

'I'm not even trying to breast feed. So you'll be able to share.'

Even the entry of the curvaceous nurse didn't alter the glaze in Andrew's eyes. He wandered to the window to look at a baby-less landscape.

Pru looked wonderingly at Andrew since his attention was elsewhere. There were four more versions of him now. At the age of twenty months Natalie had five brothers while Malcolm would have to get used to the idea that he wasn't unique.

The new four were called Colin, Curtis, Grant and Gordon. The hospital kept Pru in for three weeks until even the smallest was strong enough to go home. After collecting the bulk of his family, Andrew sat and stared at all the white bundles. Four Moses baskets lay on the through-lounge floor. Natalie hung on his knee looking at them, dummy in her mouth. Malcolm carried on playing with his train track. He was used to his sister's dolls lying around.

Pru, holding four little bottles, just warmed, stared unbelievingly at all her family. Natalie seemed absolutely huge. Then the crying began.

Chuckles were very prompt. They came the next morning, together with the local newspaper, for the first picture of all the babies at home. The newspaper had already photographed Pru on their first day, lying in her hospital bed trying to smile and Andrew holding the two strongest babies. The other two were held by a beaming nurse, displaying all the confidence of a successful hospital. She'd come from the agency an hour before.

Chuckles stayed four hours, through six bottles, four nappy changes and several bouts of fevered crying. One of the crew tried holding Grant but soon handed him back as Pru brought in the second tray of coffee and biscuits. They were quite thoughtful people although unsuccessful at getting any of the babies to look at the neonate black/white stimulation posters. Natalie was fascinated by them and kept pointing to the designs. Unfortunately, she was in the way and neither a quad nor a neonate, so she was smiled at and pushed aside.

She only cried a little, and that quietly, which was just as well since it was some fifty minutes before Pru could get to attend to her at all. Then it was only to change her and put her in the cot for a rest.

Chuckles was disappointed that Andrew was not there to hold two of the babies for their feeds while Pru held the other two. She explained that Andrew was at work and the quads didn't feed at the same time. Colin and Grant were on three-hour schedules, Gordon and Curtis were on two-hour schedules. 'What about nappy changes?' asked the young photographer, stroking his goatee beard. 'Does that happen all together?'

'It happens,' said Pru between gritted teeth, 'whenever I can get to them or whenever one of them screams hard enough.' She was by now a little rattled. She was hungry, having breakfasted at five, and she did not fancy making sandwiches for everyone. Chuckles left her, if not in peace.

Later, lots of baby equipment came the quadruplets' way. Each baby had his own cot, toiletries, toys, babygrows. The adverts allowed all the baby-owning public in the country to become thoroughly familiar with Gordon, Colin, Grant and Curtis. Pru's every foray from the house was halted by well-wishers and the curious for, after all, multiple babies are a curious sight.

Because Natalie was still only a baby herself, the pram had to allow for four babies and a seated toddler. Chuckles arranged for one to be especially designed. As with a spacecraft, it immediately attracted attention and ensured that Pru could never 'pop down to the shops' or, in fact, 'pop' anywhere. When the cameras came out, Natalie quickly learned to duck her head. It saved asking for her to be moved so that all the quads were in focus.

Malcolm was at nursery school. The health visitor had got him a free place together with the special- needs children. 'Well he has got special needs,' she justified herself.

'Oh? I hadn't thought of Malcolm like that,' Pru said.

'Most children not yet three are the centre of their parents' attention. Mums are starting to play little card games, jigsaws, even teaching them to read. Malcolm has to share his adults with Natalie and four new babies, after all. He'll need the stimulation of nursery school, won't he? He really needs it.'

Pru looked at Malcolm in the bath one night. She'd had to leave him twice already to check on urgent crying, which turned out to be Gordon who had brought up his feed. He was the poorest feeder, although not the smallest. He didn't seem to like milk.

Malcolm played with his plastic boats and a plastic bottle that had spurted water on to the bathroom floor. Pru mopped it up and tried to smile at him. He was almost like a stranger. He was at nursery school every day. She couldn't even take him there. Andrew's mother called round to do that.

Andrew's parents had been really good. They had moved house to live near the family. 'You poor girl. You're worn out with all these babies,' they said. 'We're going to sleep over one night a week and do the night feeds between us. Give you at least one night's sleep.'

'That will be wonderful,' Pru said, thankfully.

'Of course, that wouldn't have been possible if you'd been breast-feeding as the babies deserve,' said her mother. 'But still . . .'

Pru rapidly left the room, one baby under each arm, leaving her mother to look regretfully at the other two.

Andrew arrived home and looked in at each of his children although he confused Curtis with Gordon, whom he looked at twice. He brought Natalie into the bathroom from her playpen. Her nose was running. 'Can you see to this big baby?' Andrew said.

Pru saw to her. Natalie had her arms tight round her father's neck. She had just begun to make word-like sounds, rather late perhaps. 'Her sounds aren't that clear, are they?' Andrew said.

'The Health Visitor says to spend time reading to her now, and talking to her as much as possible. I'm just so tired.'

'Mm. We'd better make sure you don't fall again. Heaven knows how we'll cope once the Chuckles money stops.'

Andrew had grown tired of the jocular remarks at work. Even the novelty of having pints bought for him had worn off once he realised that he had over-proved his virility and was now the object of workmates' sympathy.

He told her, 'Pills have let us down. You'd better get the coil or something. You're obviously extremely fertile.'

'Hey! You said it was down to you. They're your genes, remember. You could have the snip.'

Andrew placed his brogues either side of the plastic train set. He glared at her. 'No way!'

Natalie's second birthday arrived. Andrew and his parents looked after all six children while Pru stole a rare hour and a half to buy Natalie a birthday present. She took the opportunity to visit the doctor for contraceptive advice. He'd received the genetic information they needed from the specialist.

'Apparently there is a distinct risk of another multiple birth if you get pregnant. How would you feel about that?'

'Desperate. I can't manage now. I simply *can't* have any more babies. Give me whatever is safest.'

'Probably the vasectomy for your husband is safest.'

'He won't.'

'Then you must both accept the degree of risk.'

Pru returned home with a prescription, the doctor's words ringing in her ears. 'This won't do for a lifetime, you know, and it isn't guaranteed like the vasectomy. We'll review it in a year or so.'

If the quads hadn't made night-times stressful, the fear of pregnancy did. Andrew mostly went to bed at a different time from Pru, lolling on the sofa for an hour with a couple of cans and the *Match of the Day* recorded, sometimes over a week old. She often flopped out on the bed after the last feed without even cleaning her teeth.

Pru accepted any help from any quarter.

Her parents were frequent visitors over the months. They would sit and look at all the babies. 'It's wonderful, really. All these babies. All yours. After the way you ate, all your life,' her mother remarked. It was almost as if she suspected Pru of snaffling the babies from shopping trolleys.

'It's a huge expense for you both, Prunella,' her father said, 'and a tight squeeze in this flat. How will you manage once the babies are out of their Moses baskets?'

'Andrew's getting a licence for that empty house in Lorgan Street, to run a nursery. We've got the equipment after all, and I certainly have the experience.' Pru knew she sounded tired rather than confident, and felt it. 'After training, we can take in twelve babies with enough staff in that building, in addition to our own. Plus there's a very large living area upstairs and a good garden.'

'You really love babies, dear, don't you?'

Her mother's tone suggested that her own loving had been satiated.

As the nursery idea took shape, Pru began to see a future.

Pru's mother cooked meals for all of them sometimes, an activity that escalated over the following months while the babies learned to roll over, Malcolm learned to somersault, and Natalie learned to understand words. She watched her grandmother carefully as she gave out advice.

'Eat up, Prunella. You must keep your strength up. All these babies to look after.'

This command was extended to Natalie. 'I hope you're going to eat up, Natalie. We want you to grow up to be a big strong girl. Leaving your meat! Wasting those carrots! You'll never grow up to have babies, mind.'

'Don't like meat. Don't like carrots.'

'You're not a good eater up, then. Oh dear, come on. You've left lots on your plate. You won't get babies.'

Pru's father leaned towards Natalie's high chair. 'You don't want to listen to your Grandma. She gets things wrong sometimes.'

'Nonsense! Eat your carrots, Natalie, yum-yums.'

Natalie glared at the plate of food, her hands on her lap.

'Tut, tut. No babies.'

Natalie regarded all her brothers on their changing mats, kicking and crying. She gave her grandmother a long look and knocked several pieces of carrot on the Afghan rug. Her words rang out clearly: 'I don't like babies. I don't like them ever.'

Three months later and the nursery is open. There are Pru's five younger children astride plastic vehicles, plus two neighbouring tots placed by parents curious to have them alongside quadruplets, and four babies of mothers desperate to get back to work. Financially, the nursery is quickly a success. Emotionally, it gives

Pru more time and space without it seeming that she is short-changing her children.

They grow up healthy, these five young men, acquire wives and babies, testament to eating up. As does the one daughter, the health economist, who lives in a South Bank loft and avoids male friends who want a lasting commitment.

'But darling,' Pru wails, 'if you don't commit soon, you'll never have babies.'

Oh, those wretched carrots, she thinks. *This is all Mother's fault.*

LAMENT

WHEN

will I be free?
When the phone stops ringing
When the babe's not clinging
When they're toilet trained
When I'm much less strained
When the sun is high
When the washing's dry
When the freezer's empty
When the dog's had plenty
When the plants are watered
When the shelves are sorted
When I've baked these hams
When they've done their exams
When the chores are done
When the kids are gone
When the in-tray's clear
When far is near
When it's not so cold
When silver's gold
When flights are cheap
When his love is deep
When I know he's free
When I'm sure it's me
When there's sign of sun
When done is done

THEN

FIRST FEAST

Elfreda watches as Mama sighs. 'How much has been lost forever!'

But with the world war two years past, the Hampstead home still holds one elaborate possession: a huge oval mirror, its frilly cream frame edged with gold. She's reflected in it, skinny little child, fingering a pink satin garment, half made. It was once a nightdress. Mama holds it open and Elfreda slides inside like a fish into its shimmering skin. 'Oooh. Ohh!'

Mama, a svelte brunette who promises to be in her prime for many years, swirls her child around then holds her still while looking deeply into the mirror. She shifts her focus from her own arched eyebrows to her daughter's pencil-box body. 'Your dress. Feel its shape, darling. It's going to be beautiful.'

Elfreda wriggles. She strokes her hands down its so-shiny surface. It sheers over her hip bones. Mama looks long at their reflections but mostly her own. (People say she's entrancing.)

'Mama?'

'I'm looking at how you'll be, poppet, when you're grown.'

Elfreda, doubtful, considers their two forms. They're not alike. If only she could be the dress.

Mama kisses her lightly on the head and trips away for lunch with friends, already perfumed, powdered and lipsticked. Her utility clothes are perked up with trimmings. Daddy's wartime parachute has provided material for an elaborate blouse. She waves to Elfreda from the landing, then disappears. Only a waft of *4711* is left as the seams on her nylons scissor downstairs.

Mama never returns. The friends' car crashes on the way to Cavendish Square, all its occupants killed outright or nearly. Father is speechless, useless. He works longer hours at the bank, engages a nanny. The pink dress lies on the bed where Mama left it, pinned at the seams.

The nanny is blonde and her accent difficult to understand. The college taught her to maintain strict rules, to be strait-laced. Elfreda is in no state to rebel. She looks at Nanny's hard back, her spiky fingers and wonders if Nanny will ever have children herself.

Winter sets in terribly. 1947 is the longest and worst on record. Everyone says so. The snow is so deep it comes over the top of Elfreda's wellies and soaks her knitted socks, freezing her toes on her way to school. At bedtime she slides into icy sheets and lies like a stick, waiting to be warmed. There is no-one who thinks about hot water bottles. Nanny has most evenings off – and out. A neighbour looks in on Elfreda at half-hour intervals until Father comes home or the clock chimes nine and the child is asleep.

By spring, Father has decamped with the now un-laced nanny. The spinster aunt, Mama's favourite sister, lands in loco parentis. She cares for Elfreda in her draughty apartment where leisure hours are spent on chaises longues contemplating the ceiling roses, the plaster foliage and fluting urns, Acanthus leaves and garlands of flowers.

For her eighth birthday a special effort is made for the bereaved child. Elfreda sits in her convent kilt hedged around by three aunts, two uncles, and two reluctant teenage cousins. It is nearly a year since her mother died, three months since her father left. He has sent a large card and a small cheque.

In front of the gathered few is a pale feast prepared by the spinster aunt: milk, ham sandwiches, cream cheese crackers, vanilla junket, meringues, and a white-iced angel cake with eight pink candles.

An uncle has bought Elfreda a scooter. One cousin has made a *I am 8* badge from cardboard and poster paint. The spinster aunty says, 'Put on your badge, Elfie. You can scoot down the road.'

Elfreda clutches a hand to her abdomen. 'I can't! People will *see* me. I can't ride a scooter. I can't wear a badge *outside*.' She stands stock still, agonised, unheeding both encourage-ments and disparagements.

The other cousin offers comfort and rescue. She opens a ludo set. 'Come on, Elfreda. I'll play you a game.'

They throw the dice as the adults pronounce sotto voce:

'Inhibited.'

'It's that prissy convent school.'

'Shhh – after losing her mother like that,'

'And her father like *that* . . .

'Sshh!'

'. . . shy . . .'

'Indulged.'

'Deprived.'

'Inhibited – as I already said!'

'We should do something . . .'

'Oh dear. Yes, I suppose . . .'

It takes four years of such urging before the aunt in charge succumbs and removes Elfreda from the care of the nuns. By now the country has emerged from dinge. There is branded washing powder and margarine, bright clothes from C&A,

refrigerators, portable gramo-phones, fresh sing-along music.

The family locate a school which promises to 'free the child'. The Janes, Annes and Marys, companions of Elfreda's past, will be replaced by Melodies, Mirabelles and Tatianas.

The new term arrives. Elfreda has not even eaten her cornflakes before she has to leave the safety of home. She clings to her aunt. 'But I won't know anyone.'

'Dearest, you soon will.'

She is greeted in Reception by a tall teacher with distracted hair who dismisses the aunt peremptorily. Elfreda, too fearful to look upwards, only sees the veined ankles in black flatties as the teacher pronounces her fate.

'You're in 2-D, Freda.'

The mistake over her name unnerves her further. She turns to run after her aunt but a firm hand on her back propels her toward a thin, paint-streaked door which displays a mosaic of multi-coloured finger prints and tattered scrawled notices. She stands trembling before it, the firm hand still at her back.

'It's Art first on your timetable. Your set are in there. In you go.' The hand pushes. 'Straight in.'

Gawky Elfreda guesses the impact she will make on her new class, although she doesn't predict from what angle she will make it. Lying in a circle on their stomachs, twenty-six twelve-year-olds swivel their fifty-two inquisitors' eyes upwards to take in the fawn pallor, saggy uniform, bony knees and baby Clarks sandals that is Elfreda. The class is arranged head-first around a concentric array of colourful foods.

It is like a brilliant illustration from a book she's never seen. Elfreda's feet feel anchored to the spot, her mouth open to the elements.

'Lie down!' welcomes Mrs Skop, glorious in puce flowers and golden locks. Elfreda's gazelle legs quiver, flex and finally give way as she sinks on to her stomach. She lies prone beside the others, her eyes level with darkly baked sausage rolls, livid salami, cheeses spotted with ochre, orange, blue/grey – and carrots, celery sticks, viscous grapes, raisins, bright red apples, blood red cherries, chocolate fingers, powdery marshmallows and meringues, glinting lime jelly, date loaf, ginger tea -bread and sugary pink cakelets.

'The idea,' explains Mrs Skop gorgeously, 'is to eat your way from the outside to the inside of the circle.'

'How wide across can we eat?' asks a plump child, Amanda, raring to go.

'Imagine a wedge. Eat your way through to the apex. Go wild,', she says to the children who have only known wartime rations. 'Experience with all of your senses: see, smell, touch, lick. Eat as much as you like, smarm your faces, sink your teeth in, stick your fingers in, stuff your mouths, gobble it all up. Listen to the eating sounds – yours and everyone else's – gobble, guzzle, slurp, smack, swallow, burp.' She pauses while gasps and giggles, minor explosions, confirm that the girls have relished her words. 'And when I give the signal – *gorge*.'

Mrs Skop's gaze alights upon the two glistening orbs which differentiate the paralysed newcomer from the surrounding brown uniforms. 'You particularly, child. Let loose your inhibitions. Free yourself. Ready?' She stands back and blows a whistle.

The gobbling up begins.

Mrs Skop stands upon the remains of a stage and surveys the surging mass of pubescent pupils experiencing a last chomp at childhood. The gentle heaving of the skirts circling around the foodstuffs resembles a billowing parachute landing in a field of plenty.

'Come *on!*' Mrs Skop, striding forward, urges Elfreda whose pitiful grazing – a nervous nibbling, a choking swallow – make a still spot in the vibrant host of worker bees.

More fearful of Mrs Skop than the food, Elfreda crams in a meringue and scatters a snow shower with her panicky breathing. Not to be defeated, Mrs Skop grasps a banana, places Elfreda's limp fingers around it and tears off the peel. 'Pretend it's the first time you've seen one. Take a large bite. Glory in it.'

(Indeed, Elfreda did encounter her first banana only a year ago. With excited eyes her aunt had held it out. It had curved around Elfreda's hand. Tentatively she'd licked it. 'No!' the cousins had chortled. 'You peel it, *then* eat it.')

Mrs Skop loses patience with Elfreda's nibbling. She grabs the small hand and squeezes it around the banana until the white liquid runs through the skinny fingers. 'Now lick them. Delicious!' Then she turns to survey the heaving host.

The serious sounds of gorging drown Elfreda's whimpers as she feeds from the crumbs on her plate. Surreptitiously she slides a hanky from the elastic of her brown knickers and removes the remains of banana and meringue. She eyes the vandalised feast.

The array had been an artistic glory, a land of beauty. The class has attacked and now it's a carnage. The host have been loyal to their teacher's inspiring call to gorge. Only crumbs lie where piles of cakes stood, smears where there were spreads. The reds and oranges, the purples and greens have all turned to brown, merging with the school uniform. Eventually the urgent activity slows and ceases. There are grunts, sighs and burps and worse.

'*And now,*' calls Mrs Skop, 'Stand, and take up your brushes. I want you to paint – Gluttony.'

Blank sheets of sugar paper await them, sellotape-slapped on to the walls.

Elfreda, her past artistic experience: *Mummy, A House, A Daffodil*, looks at her empty little hand wiped clean of food. Mrs Skop thrusts into it a gross bristle brush. A patty pan of primary colours stands beside her together with a full beaker. Elfreda dips a tentative bristle into the water.

Mrs Skop grasps Elfreda's forearm and plunges it into the red paint. 'Gluttony!' she breathes, urging Elfreda's fingers with their sticky brush-load on to the hungry sugar paper.

The brush trembles as Elfreda lets the hairs touch the paper, wondering what 'gluttony' means. Her paint strokes fade to a streak as weak as Elfreda's desire.

All around her well-fed girls, free girls, successful girls, happy girls, have set to with thickly-covered brushes, and created wondrous feasts on their receptive canvases. Some use their food-smeared hands and faces to represent Gluttony, that abstract noun their first feast has inspired. These spontaneous and vivid excrescences are displayed on the wall by an ecstatic Mrs Skop. She has created her own retribution for all those years of want. At the day's end, Elfreda's faint paint trails hang miserably beside her peers' masterpieces.

That night she dreams. She's being held down by a huge Mrs Slop who is made of jelly, chips and chocolate. She thrusts armfuls of food into the prised-open mouth of Elfreda, whose clenched teeth make feeble resistance.

'Open yourself! Relish the experience!' she urges, and in go all the foods in a sickly mass. With sticky hands this Mrs Slop thrusts scarlet and puce paint, the bristly brushes, the host of brown- uniformed girls, the piles of books, the registers, the art room, the whole school towards the shrinking child.

'What a feast!' enthuses Mrs Slop as she stuffs Elfreda, ready to display her on the wall.

Elfreda's little hands waver desperately before her mouth to prevent the vast mass from entering and overwhelming her. Then she awakes, her throat aching, her legs stretched thinly down her single wooden bed with its starched sheets.

In adulthood, Elfreda is no longer a gazelle. She lays the credit at Mrs Skop's door for introducing her to colour, expression, involvement, sensation. Throughout her adolescence, Elfreda befriends food. Food: sweet, savoury, spicy, succulent, she longs to smell it, smear it, swallow it. While guzzling and gorging, she feels successful, someone who has loosed her inhibitions. It is as though her acts of greed will be applauded.

And now, fresh from her bath, Elfreda surveys her today self in the beautiful oval mirror, her one inheritance from the past. Botticelli or Rubens might load their brushes to describe her buoyant buttocks. Glazed thighs, luscious beyond peaches or mangoes, slap together as she moves. Who would not want to smooth their fingers along their dimpled surface, sink their hands in, or their mouths, their tongues, their teeth? What a feast of a body!

Elfreda contemplates the outline she has filled in fleshily, from top to toe. She smooths her hands down her satiny self, listening for those longed-for words: 'You're lovely, darling!'

Sad that Mama cannot see how she has grown.

Elfreda's eyes linger over her body. She longs to grasp a handful and thrust it into her mouth. If she pinched an inch, might it slide through her fingers, disappearing like a magician's silk handkerchief? Could she take her flesh off, like a pink satin dress, and leave it behind on the bed unpinned?

She shudders. No. This body is for display. There are no marks on her marshmallow skin and when she leaves the house she'll wear no bra, no corset under her flowing dress. The class shall see her body in its perfect state. She is the most prized of the Art College's models. In an hour, they will be seated, brushes raised, all eyes upon her.

But before becoming their rich re-creation, she must first feast. She hurries to the pure white fridge where a new batch of profiteroles lies in waiting.

Her mouth opens, ready for the light pastry upon her tongue. For this moment, she is alone, the weight of the days behind and before her.

A SLIGHT INVASION

Daryl's in the hall, waiting. She drums up images of hideous things so that anything about to happen will seem milder.

Fish. She shudders. Dying slowly, smelly scaly fish squirming close enough to slither on her skin, the largest one fixing her with its black-rimmed eye, riveting her to its agony. (Mother, Aunty, Grandad: 'Eat it up, it's good brain food.') As bad as eating a brain, soggy, grey-pink, wriggling against her tongue, forcing its fishy thoughts past her epiglottis.

She's always hated fish and soon she'll be at the fish market with every kind of them.

Then the post delivers itself through the slit in the door. Plop — like a fish leaping on to dry land. Two letters. Now something belongs to her.

She's already dressed and coated, ready for the off. She picks them up.

One is the usual franked envelope, same size and slimness as before. She knows too well what it will contain. The other one's some card or other trivia. She opens her bag, puts them in. She must leave the house now.

She's planned this exodus. She planned where she'd go, where she'd come to terms with her loss. She doesn't want Howard a witness to her distress, increasing his own. It is far better she is out if he should be coming downstairs from the bedroom after-shaved, or out of the kitchen, bone china cup and saucer in his hand.

Daryl knows how she'll feel as soon as the confirmation comes. She has to get to a place where Howard certainly will not be, to buy something she knows he'll love.

Although face it, Howard is not either in bed or in the kitchen. He is gone elsewhere. Even his body odour, damp, spiced, sweet and sour.

Once he used to call her 'Light of his life' – not that long ago, in years. His face would light up as he saw her descend fresh from the train after work, eager for their long, homely evenings together: cooking, tie-dying, cross-wording.

She loved his sleek hair, his perfect shape like a model in a tailor's window. And she loved feeling loved, chosen for his design. He bought her wedding dress, arranged her, prepared her, shop-windowed her to make her perfect.

She swanned out on the day, buffeting taffeta down the aisle. She saw his evaluating glance at her tiered hair and cast down her eyes enhanced with the silvered mascara he had bought her. She smiled downwards, he'd know it was for him. He, the bridegroom, smooth, perfectly adorned: a Ken of a man. Daryl was eager to play-act Barbie. Howard appraised her performance, taking her on as if he believed her real.

And it was fun. He tickled her. She tickled him and made him squeal. It was exhilarating to know his sensitive zones. He was cross about this loss of dignity and would try to get her back, but she slipped by him, taunting. She loved his face getting red, sophistication slipping away from his control.

They didn't have children. They were each other's children. They played. They chased each other, flicking wet tea towels, chuckling like children. It was Howard's way of comforting her.

Daryl had tried to get pregnant. They had the tests. They were told whose body was dysfunctional. They both looked after her afterwards.

She grew depressed. Howard tactfully withdrew. He didn't want to invade her feelings.

Time passed. Howard said he'd spend more time away from the house, not to burden her. She grew over-light from the increasing absence of his burden. He stayed more absent than present. She didn't blame him. She could hardly bear to look at him, bereft. Poor Howard crushed by disappointment. She felt almost sadder for him than for herself. No wonder he kept away from their cosy evenings knowing he was not to be a daddy, not to have a little light in his life.

When Daryl had a daddy, he'd read to her from the *Arabian Nights*. 'Who will change old lamps for new?'

Who indeed? The doctors can't.

She draws breath. As she moves through the front door she looks at the hall-stand where Howard keeps a clothes brush, a long comb, a shoe-shine pad, and mascara and lipstick (for her). It has a large mirror. Her hair is cut and graded around her grave face, the blank eyes dark. She stares at them. This old lamp had been the light of her husband's life. Now it seems snuffed out.

She leaves, walking up the neat road as if she is like any other woman. Tip tap, tip-top. Her shoes are brick red, shiny, a post-natal hue.

She knows the many procedures for helping couples' fertility. Each they've tried and each has culminated in a brief letter: *Dear Mrs Burrows, I regret to inform you . . . tests proved negative.* Daryl is so used to their regret, the franked envelope. Who would bother to lick a stamp for her?

After the word 'unfortunately' she doesn't read on. Something happens to people working in large organizations. And a white coat tippexes their personality.

Daryl's own doctor, always uncoated, is a sweetie. She used to have photos on her desk of her four exotic children, fleshy and full of vitality. Those haven't been seen lately. She probably puts them in a drawer when it's Daryl's appointment. She knows how Daryl yearns for a little hand to push itself into hers. It shows in her face. She'd surely give Daryl one of her children if she could part with one. Can you — if you have four? Probably not. Only if the baby wasn't really yours.

Howard says too much fuss is made about babies. There are 'Other Things in Life'. Bravely, he is letting her down lightly. Her heart twists with sorrow for him.

Recently they made one last ditch, expensive attempt. Howard tried to dissuade her, trying to do without Daddiness so she wouldn't have to suffer further. But she worked over-time to show him she was really trying her very best to be a fulfilling wife, a lamp to his future.

After the appointment, awkward and embarrassing as ever, Howard took her for a wonderful meal in a French restaurant. He nearly had fish, but he didn't. Howard loves fish, his favourite meals are all fish.

Daryl has waited for the post many days, imagining the envelope lying delivered, the upturned smile of its flap licked shut, awaiting her with its finality. It will convey to Howard that she is to be his only child forever.

The fish market is the last place on earth he will look for her, the fuss she always makes over the smell of fish.

'Don't bring it in here!', she squeals. 'Gut it down the end of the garden, wrap it up in film, put it in this dish and put the lid on. Then you can bring it in.' She's not joking, Howard knows it.

'Don't touch me, I can still smell fish on your hands!'

'But I've washed them twice in your antibacterial!'

'I can smell fish. Uggghh!'

After they'd been married a while, Howard converted to fish fingers and breaded haddock, dry and chewy, but hardly smelly at all.

No-one needs directions to the fish market. Daryl's nose takes her; her shoes beacon the way. Outside, she breathes in enough air for a dozen people and holds it tight before she goes in.

The fish market is an alternative social experience, a full range of human expression laid out on slabs. There's ling, like herself: grey, inert, condemned, her lights put out. Salmon for Howard, primped and frilled, ready for the table, at a price. Dogfish for his parents ('Time doesn't stand still, you know'); skate for hers (flatly, 'You always have your career'); mackerel for the diminishing number of childless friends; and sardines for the child-bearing ones ('Come round later when our little terrors are in bed'); sprats for all the offspring of all the friends.

There's the shocked cod, mouth agape. Haddock, its silver-coiled lips neatly closed, down-turns them disdainfully: *'Ugh, humans! Don't you just hate the smell of them?!'* Little whingeing whitebait, still wriggling, strut their silver. Tuna, so big and moist, display such painfully human flesh, ecstatic John Dory with mascara-ringed eyes. Next to them there's something foreign, unnamed, staggered to be lying on crushed ice below the glinting knife of the filleter. Then some dogfish with their sharp shark eyes. Once, in childhood, on the beach, Daryl trod hard on one. Out slid a baby fish, so easily. Both dead, they lay side by side wasted on the pebbles, the baby delivered by Daryl's careless foot.

She breathes in, covering her mouth with her scarf, grasping her handbag. She must prepare herself to leave this place, meet her husband and bring him home to face up to the childless situation. She will soften it with a capitulation, a beautifully baked fish. Which to choose? She walks around the fish market, returns the empty fishy gazes. She casts her eyes across the market for a long fish-filled view, breathing into her scarf all the while.

At the far end two men close together, are absorbed in choosing their fish. One of them so familiar. Her husband. Here? The other unfamiliar – a colleague? Daryl doesn't know the young man with the smooth cheeks and dimpled chin, the ruffed haircut.

Howard clearly knows him well. Very well, for he takes the young man's hand and looks at it, tenderly. The palm is pink, rosy like poached trout. The tasty bite, so long forbidden by fish-phobic wife.

Howard chooses and pays for two sole, and the pair look at each other, smiling, perhaps discussing how they will cook their fish tonight when Howard is busy not burdening Daryl with his presence.

Her first instinct is to hide. She draws her scarf over her head as if it is she who has done something shameful. She supposes she has – being female, infertile, even her orifices not the ones Howard prefers.

She looks down and feigns a concentrated pose, fluttering her hands inside her bag. The letters give her the perfect excuse to busy herself there. They aren't opened yet. Since she knows what the contents of one will be, she opens the other first.

A pretty card congratulates her on her expected baby. Some sick joke, some vicious, deranged neighbour? But no – it's from her doctor, expressing absolute delight at Daryl's hard-won success. It's sincere, so is she misinformed? The doctor encloses ante-natal information. Has the unbelievable really happened?

She tears angrily at the other letter, from the hospital, with its poor quality fudgy print, her name misspelled. It tersely confirms the news. Objective as ever, dead-pan, uncaring, factual, whether reporting wondrous or unbearable news. Daryl reads it four times, just in case. Yes, it's true. It is true.

Daryl sits down.

The chair belongs to the stall-holder. She stands up. She is alive. Every particle of her is glistening.

Now she should be full of shrieking excitement, faith and belief restored a thousand-fold. She should be rushing out to rape her man and champagne the world as he has champagned her reluctant ovaries.

She looks up with her genie's eyes across the fish market. She sees that champagne will not bubble for her for Howard, Daddy, is walking off, holding his fish in one hand and his lover's in the other. He has his two delights, one of them secret. Howard moves away from his old lamp with his new, like the John Dory, ecstatic.

Howard, the lamp-changer, has swapped his fish finger for a sole.

Eventually Daryl unfreezes, like a displayed fish lifting itself off the slab. Her glance falls upon a bed of chipped ice and vivid plastic grass. She buys a freezer pack of prawns, odourless. She'll never eat them. She takes her pack to the steps leading from the fish market out into the sunshine, away from the stench.

A newspaper stand offers distraction. She buys a paper and takes it to a café. She sits with it open holding a coffee cup, a woman celebrating her triumph over infertility.

On page four: *Recent government-funded research reveals that 50 per cent of male downstream river fish have changed their sex.* How? Why? The waste from human fertile females washes their contraceptives into the rivers and seas, converting fish males who would father into females who choose not to mother. Why should Daryl struggle against the tide?

She drains her coffee and goes home with her pretty card from the sweetie of a doctor who has visualised Daryl's delight. It stands on her mantelpiece where it is destined to gather the dust of the weary months awaiting her fatherless child. Her doctor has inscribed the expected date. *February 14th. How romantic!!* It's bound to be late. For in a few days it will be a Pisces. Of course it will be a Pisces. She remembers the sign's characteristics: Pisceans are escapists.

Come February, against her contractions, that yearned-for nub will swim his slippery slide down her channels to be beached on to the white slab of delivery table. He'll wriggle free from her body and into her everyday life.

But will she know him as her own, or will she recognize sturgeon, John Dory or trout? Her baby, of whom she had dreamed, was to be born from the giggling, chasing, tickling, the loved plaything of loving Ken and Barbie.

This infant has been conceived expensively, his existence confirmed and realised in a fish market, the most impossible place for his mother, to be. She learned of him at the very moment she saw his father's betrayal. The baby can't be hers. This child is more the product of fish-lovers.

Daryl's wail rings out, wrenched from her gullet, wracking the walls. She clutches her stomach and rolls on the floor, legs together, thrashing. She's like a fish without water. There is no-one to hear, so she wails her throat dry until the last vestiges trail away and her body twitches, shudders.

Then she struggles up, scrabbles in her desk, finds pen, paper. She writes Howard a note:

> *Congratulations to you both.*
> *Amazingly, there is to be a baby.*
> *Prepare your celebration.*
> *He will be ready for you in February.*
> *Collect him any time; he's hardly mine.*

She doesn't sign it. Her name seems unimportant.

THE REAL PRIZE

Over the pints I learned that Des had paired off with Sylvia.

'You're kidding.'

'I'm not, Ricky. They're an item.'

'*Sylvia*. He must be desperate.'

Beefy put his word in. 'Shucks, that'll be a silent affair, haw haw haw.'

'Not going to work, is it? I mean . . .' I was out of words.

I'd always seen old Des as a loser, although in some ways we'd been neck and neck during our school days. And he never had the style to pull the birds. But Sylvia – no-one would have wished that on him. There's nothing against her, mind. She was always turned out well and could have been quite a looker. Except she was deaf and dumb. You couldn't say anything she'd hear, and she couldn't say a thing, not a sound. Been like that since she was five years old. Tragedy. Tragedy for the whole family. Real shame, all sympathies, but obviously you weren't going to date her. But now, word was, Des was.

We used to sit together in Science, back in our school days. Des did the recording, I did the experiments. He borrowed my biro. I cadged his notes, forgot to give them back. I won the Science prize, great trip to Greenwich Observatory. I'd never been anywhere *near* London before.

Des was a pale lad then, and long-faced, last to be chosen when we needed teams.

After school, I got a job in the printing works for starters. So did Des. I was an apprentice, he was a runner – a gofer. A year later, he was still a runner and I'd got a job on the local rag, moved to the county town.

Well, - you know the rest about me. I won't brag.   I lived well, kept my old friends. People liked that. Said it showed I had no side. Success hadn't spoiled me.

Failure hadn't spoiled Des, either.

He was useful to the print works. They relied on him to know where everything was; to be there, same place, same face.

'Oi, Des! Where's the bleeding this, that, the other? Oi, Des, any mail, tea, print-outs, cardboard cartons, new pens, paper clips, ashtrays? I can't find the whosit, the whatsit. Where is it? Dunno. Ask Des. Hey, Des!'

I reckon Des felt important. He was needed in that way.

Sylvia didn't feel important. She was taken on at the print works under that government scheme, E.O. The firm needed to show it was committed to Equality of Opportunity, yeah, disabled people can have a chance of dogsbody jobs too. But Sylvia knew the score. In the print room there was always a high level of noise. It got you down. But Sylvia didn't even know that it was there.

She was a nice enough person, given the obvious.

When the lads told me Des was dating her, I reckoned he'd just take her out a few times to please his mother – she was always going on at him to 'get a nice girl-friend'. So I shrugged. Wouldn't actually harm him.

Then I was sent to the city, upgraded. For fourteen glorious months, I drove around in my Morgan, roof back, Babette's gingery curls blowing high and tangling as we raced along between restaurants, night clubs, events and parties. I swanned around, Babette on my arm, showing off my prize.

When I got home next I found that Des had married Sylvia. The lads were full of it.

It'd been a small and simple wedding, but everyone came to the church gates. Novelty, I suppose. I could imagine the oldies gawping at the couple from outside and wishing them well as they threw confetti. I'd missed it. Poor old Des. I guess he'd have liked me there and I hadn't even left him an email address. Still, I went straight round to see them. Bought them a white telephone with a brass bell and a Mickey Mouse handle.

No surprise to hear that Des was still at the print works, and so was Sylvia, but now only part-time. She was busy developing her home. Des and his mother scraped together some bit of a mortgage, or may be Sylvia's mum put some to it. God knows, the old girl must have been thrilled to have a man come into Sylvia's life.

My mother muttered that you couldn't make a silk purse out of a sow's ear. Wasn't sure whether she meant him or her.

The women at our local said Sylvia bought home improvement magazines and made things like lychee mousse, swagged curtains and sprigged tablecloths. She did a correspondence course in commercial law. So she must have been bright enough.

Her visitors came back saying how Sylvia had cooked this, made this, painted that; Sylvia and Des had created a balcony, a patio, a through room. People started seeking her advice on furnishings and style.

Remember that nursery story about Griselda who was locked away with piles of straw to spin them into gold before morning? I always liked that kid's story. This stuff about Sylvia made me think of it.

We asked the happy couple to join us at the local.

Des would talk to us, but sign to her. She'd taught him how. You'd mouth to her the odd phrase and she would nod, but otherwise she'd sit quiet, watching, while everyone else jabbered away.

I told Des the Griselda story and he signed it to her. She put a hand on my arm and nodded meaningfully.

Before long, Des was starting to look quite a cool dude. Even his back seemed straighter. Sylvia was doing something about his gear, according to Des's ma. He'd certainly smartened up. Word was, Sylvia stopped Des before he left the house and point to his shoes if they weren't super-clean. She had a clothes brush by the front door. Perhaps she had a comb and hair gel too, who knows, but Des's hair got the treatment.

Who knows what else Sylvia did at the front door, but he'd arrive at the print works with the smile still stuck on his face, his chin in the air and an expression that said 'Look at me, I'm something'.

One day Des finally got pulled out of the print room and into the front office. Smart enough to face the public now, see.

It wasn't just the boss who noticed Des. I think there was a secretary there who gave him the eye. There was some gossip about people being back late after lunch break, people not using the works canteen. Who knows what was going on? But it stopped.

Des told me that if he ever *thought* of another woman, Sylvia knew. Weird. He'd let his mind stray one evening to 'someone' he'd met, wondering would there be any harm in their having a drink together. In came Sylvia with her face so black and threatening old Des felt scared. He signed, 'What?', and she signed, 'Other woman'. He made a bewildered face and she glared, unbelieving. She ignored him for four days and he had to make his own meals.

Another story circulated about the summer party at the works. Three of the temps cornered poor Des after some wager. He'd had quite a bellyful, the girls were tipsy, and after all it was three against one. Des was down in a heap with all three on top of him when they were found. A ring formed round them, cheering and making raucous comments. You know what these things are like. All good clean fun.

Sylvia was by the barbecue, serving sausages. The guys said she suddenly went rigid, dumped the pan down and strode through three rooms to where Des was just staggering to his feet, red-faced with these three pretty fillies snuggling around him. Now how did Sylvia know that?

Anyway, she made short work of everyone there. She signed, 'My husband!' No-one but Des could sign but everyone realised what she was saying. There was a lot of embarrassed explaining and mouthing. Imagine trying to explain an office dare to a deaf-mute!

Des lit out of the party, three steps behind his wife. Whatever happened next who knows, but Sylvia's hours at the print works were increased. Des's productivity went up. So he was promoted. Again. But I was off, living it up in the city.

The next time I met Des he was on a management course.

'Des!' I said, I guess in a tone of some amazement. It was six years since we'd worked together. Despite his promotions I still saw him as that gofer, a no-hoper.

We were put in the same small group. We were supposed to be learning how to maximise our individual talents in a team setting. I didn't take that one too seriously. The course meant a week off work. Alongside Des, I'd breeze along, share his notes, enjoy the hotel facilities. A jazz.

I hadn't reckoned on how confident Des had become. I'd assumed he would be my side-kick each time I made a point to the group. Instead, he bloody argued and made one of his own. In fact, Des did well good on that course.

Yeah, well, it wasn't my scene. I'm not sure that management is. I used to cope with all that striving and targets. It felt good with Babette on my arm, but to tell the truth she led me a dance. She liked the night-life, and so did I, but she could lie in mornings, lady of leisure.

When things got tough for me at work, Babette's answer was simple. 'Forget it. Chill. Let's go to a club.' She was a right clubber. I had problems. She'd put a drink in my hand. 'Get that down and you won't care so much.'

I'd have got on famously if Babette had supported me, but she got fed up and went off with Carl Grisham in a Buick. By then it was too late for me to salvage my career.

Big boss hauled me into his glass office. 'You don't roll the goods in, you don't make the grade. Sorry, Ricky, it's curtains. Have to let you go.'

And where could I go but back to the local rag which had known me in my more go-getting years? I came back at a higher level, but not with the swagger of success.

Meanwhile, Sylvia had looked after Des. She read up about super-foods and became quite a dietary expert. Des said that each time he reached for the wrong item of food, he'd get a 'feeling'. If he ignored it, he'd face a fearsome expression that night. He was clearly scared to lose whatever had stuck that smile on his face and his chin in the air.

Sylvia moved Des on to exercise. He joined a gym and got really fit. No more 'kick me' expression but a slim waist, broad chest and well-toned muscles. Along with a new car and a house with a games room, and a fireplace the size of their old patio.

In my lesser moments I wonder if Sylvia sent out silent messages to Des on that management course so that he could do and say all those neat things.

The last time I was round their place, it was to deliver a cheque for a crossword competition. It was a beefed-up promotion financed by Aeron ISA Company. You had to buy one to enter, but the prize was huge. *Englers' Encyclopaedia* provided a buff to set the clues.

Me? I never do crosswords. Beyond me, mate.

Sylvia won it. Shock enough, but what was really weird, was the solution to the tortuous clue for 9-across. Very few competitors had decoded it. *Griselda* was the answer. I looked at her, but didn't dare sign. She smiled.

Des took the cheque and gazed at his wife as if she were magic. Perhaps she was. That money was going to take them into another life-style altogether.

I should have known when I held up that Science trophy that the applause was momentary; that it was Des who would end up with the real prize.

A CHANGE OF SUPPORT

It arrived early in the morning, my new mattress. I can't remember what it's called, but I'll think of the name later. I heard a cheerful whistling and opened the door, and there it was, in the arms of a man. I was so pleased to welcome it into my world; I hadn't had a decent night's sleep for months, or so it felt.

'Oh,' I said to the delivery man, looking at the shape. 'It's in a tube.'

'S'right. Very compressed.' He stuck it on its end, beside my old bed. 'Better take your old one off, then.'

I slid it off on the other side of the bed. Poor thing, it had seen better days.

'Looks like you were more than due for this one.' He tapped the tube.

'Yes.' I was struggling with the purple packaging and tape that surrounded it. There was enough protection! You don't expect that much for something that's presumably unbreakable.

He withdrew a mean- looking pair of scissors with long points. 'I'll cut through.'

Make the incision, I thought he was going to say. But he was a down-to-earth chap.

The purple plastic bled back in a complaint of wrinkles while the extra strong white tape spread-eagled apart with a protesting snap. Underneath, the cardboard tube was revealed, shiny, with promises written on the top. *The sweetest dreams you've ever had.*

I took off the lid. I could see the head of the mattress itself in the tightest of curls.

I slid my fingers down the edge of it, one hand on each side. The mattress felt silky. I gave an attempt at a pull, fingers digging into whatever part of it I could grab. It didn't budge. It had obviously been rammed in with an instrument of immense power. My fingers had never felt so inadequate. Should I turn it the other way and push from the other end? I bent to look, but that part was very clearly not designed to be removed.

The man was leaning against my bedroom wall, arms folded.

I chanced an agonised smile. 'I'll never get it out, will I? Not on my own.'

He looked me up and down. 'Make me a cuppa and I'll lay it out for you.'

'All right.'

'Two sugars.'

When I came back from the kitchen with the tea, sugared and stirred, he had un-wrapped all the packaging and was drawing the mattress out of its tube, sliver by sliver. It was emerging from its birthing channel before my eyes. But slowly. I put the tea down silently, afraid to disturb the process.

I watched with tense hands and a tight stomach. He pulled slowly but firmly, breathing hard. More of the mattress appeared, first rolled and then trying to unfold itself. At last with a whoosh the last of the mattress landed plop upon the bed -frame.

Thrilled, I hovered as it settled, and tentatively stroked its surface.

The man had already turned to gulp at his tea. 'Phew. I needed that.'

The rest of the business was rapid. In a moment, the man had the old mattress out in my hall, together with the mess of packaging and the empty tube. 'Right then.'

The new mattress was light gold, gleaming. It was so inviting, displaying its riches. I rushed to sit on it, perhaps lie down, but the man stopped me with almost a shout.

'Don't touch it! It has to regain its proper size. It'll swell to almost double by tomorrow.'

I think my face showed my disappointment. I couldn't wait to try it out.

'You can sleep on it tonight,' he said reluctantly, 'but it won't be at its best. Tomorrow would be better.'

'Tomorrow! I don't have another bed.'

'Well, then, I shouldn't turn in until very late if I were you.'

'All right.' I confined myself to stroking its surface gently. 'It looks amazing.'

'You wait. The longer you have this, the more it'll grow on you.'

'Really?'

'No question.'

He downed the rest of his tea and, ignoring the coaster on the bedside table, plonked his mug on the Georgian table my mother had given me when I turned twenty. He obviously wanted to leave his mark.

'Your birthday, is it?' He poked his finger towards my seven birthday cards.

'Last week. Twenty-nine.'

'Mm. Around what I'd guessed. Happy Returns, Miss.'

'Thank you. And thanks very much for the extraction. It would have been completely beyond me.'

'Yes,' he said in a self-satisfied way. 'Shall I dispose of this for you?' He poked a disdainful finger at the old mattress.

'Please.' I watched him heave the old hairy thing through the door. I should have replaced it before but had just taken it for granted. I'd had it since I was a child. You could see the old blood stains from the days before I learned how to manage periods properly. I'd slept on it since I was three, so probably there were older stains too. I was glad to see it go, an uncomfortable remnant of times past.

'I'll take this down the tip for you, but you'll have to dump the wrappings yourself.'

'Of course. Thank you so much.'

'Right-o. Bye-bye. Enjoy your nights.'

The door slammed behind him. His cheery whistle soon faded to a peep. Something in my solar plexus leapt and twisted. I rushed to the window to see him heaving the mattress into his van. That lumpy old mattress had known me a third of my life so far. That's what you spend in bed, isn't it, a third? It knew intimacies forever hidden from others. I felt bad, letting it go. Like putting a dog down before it had quite died.

The van was his own, not a firm's delivery van. He had a variety of rubbish in the back. He must have been on his way to the tip anyway. I could see some branches and a pile of red dust. He was shoving some boxes out of the way so that the mattress could slide fully into the van. One edge had split. A thick curl of whitish hair sidled out like an unwanted relative. Another push and my mattress collapsed over the boxes. The van door slammed, the man started whistling again and went to his driving seat. Another slam.

I watched the van disappear around the corner. I had let my mattress go and my old self with it. Meanly, I had consigned the old support to lie with brick dust and garden refuse.

For some reason I couldn't fathom, I had a glass of white wine. It wasn't even eleven a.m.

Then I went to my bottom drawer and drew out my new white sheets encased in delicate wrappings, an unused present for a long-ago event that had never arrived. I smoothed them over the golden surface. I stood back and surveyed my virginal linen displayed on the mattress that no -one had ever lain upon. My pillows were old with saggy stuffing. I wouldn't put them on this new mattress. I took them to the kitchen. They fitted into a large carrier and I whisked them away with the mattress tube and its wrappings. I felt like the midwife with the afterbirth. Once I'd dumped them I was going to buy brand new pillows.

Casting a backward glance at the new mattress, I pulled my load out of the front door. I was as reluctant to leave as a mother with a new baby, but the mess of the arrival needed to be gone. I put on my Puffa jacket and obeyed my instincts. Out with the old, and oh, the eagerness to try the new.

Once home again with new fluffy pillows, I dithered and fussed, cleaning the already clean bedroom. The mattress was swelling, invisibly, but I knew it was readying itself for me. I read a magazine, cooked, ate, cleared up, cleaned a little more, watched TV.

Every hour or so I checked on how engorged the mattress was becoming. I waited up as long as I could, then I showered and smoothed on body lotion. Almost shyly, I slid under the sheets, wary of inhibiting my mattress's rise to perfection. I lay back gently, closed my eyes and waited to experience what the mattress had to offer.

Despite my hesitance, the mattress welcomed me upon it. Even that very first night was thrillingly comfortable.

In the morning I got up refreshed, eager to experience the next night when the mattress would have gained its full potential. I felt invigorated as well as comforted. I even sang as I got ready for work. I marched off to the office with a new vigour and didn't give anyone grief for a change.

All that had been promised was true! There aren't many events in life you can say that about.

The following nights were even more comfortable; luxurious, you well might well say. I woke in the morning with the sense that capable hands supported my body at every point. The downside was that it was difficult to get up and leave that special feeling that you have never been so supported before, that you have never felt so comfortable, and never will again.

At the office, everyone said how well I was looking these days. 'You're like a new woman. Something has obviously happened in your life . . .'

I smiled mysteriously. Let them wonder. Perhaps only I knew how bad things had been with me, about me, lately.

Since I lost Matthew I've been totally down in the dumps. Lost, did I say? It was me who left him, or rather, let him, no, *made* him leave me, but it was what everyone was saying to me that made me do it.

'Harriet, he's not letting you have any life.'

'You're being controlled.'

Listen, Harriet, I think he's a bit, well, touched.'

Afterwards, I knew I'd done the sensible thing but I did miss feeling that I was someone's most important person. I did miss all the comforts Matthew provided.

Matt was a helpful man, a giving, supportive person. From the beginning I was courted with chocolate and flowers. From my first visit to his home he seemed to find it really difficult for the evenings to end. Standing on the doorstep, he cut a tragic figure and I waved goodbye. He cooked, he brought me tea in bed when I stayed over, he was always praising me. He made me feel needed.

He was a thin person himself whose nose peered at his chin as though checking it wasn't going to disappear. There were little curls beside his ears, smaller ones inside. I never got around to asking if those could be removed. His knees were exceptionally bony. I can vouch for that because we first met in the intimate encounter that travelling on the tube in rush hour enforces. At every station, Matt either jerked against me, or I fell against him.

'So sorry,' (him.).

Bump.

'Sorry,' (me.).

At the Temple he got out, throwing a regretful glance at me once the onward moving crowd allowed an eye to eye through the closing doors. I went on to Bank and didn't expect to see him again. The London tube. It's a miracle if you see anyone twice.

The *Metro* newspaper sorts that problem out. In the Love or Lust section that week, Matt put, *'To the voluptuous lady who damaged my feet at the Temple, please meet me outside station, 7 p.m. Dinner with me is your punishment.'*

Although I was bruised along my thigh from his bony knees, how could I resist such a public message?! It was utterly charming.

Matt always said he liked my curves. He must have done, for his way of treating me added to them. Every time we met, he greeted me with chocolates. Every time I went to his home, a three-course gourmet meal awaited me.

'Do have some more poulet a la crème, snapper Veracruz, profiteroles, cheesecake, brûlée, Bailey's.'

When I hesitated, his expression was so agonised I hadn't the heart to refuse. Especially the cheesecake, it came in all flavours and was irresistible.

Until Matt, I'd always had girly nights. At least eight of us went to the wine bar and drank ourselves sillier than we already were. We had such a laugh. A pizza and salad, a good wine to wash it down, the comedy house to follow. I have to admit it was fun. Whether we were single, or wives having a night off, we set each other off with office gossip, male impersonations, risqué jokes that got steadily riskier as the meal progressed and the drinks were topped up.

After Matt, I stopped going with the girls. At first, I'd get ready to leave as usual but he'd come to my door and say, 'You don't want to go out, do you? I've made you a genuine Italian lasagne, there's your favourite rose and a zabaglione to follow.'

He'd gone to all that trouble making a beautiful dinner. How could I leave him to spend the evening alone? And anyway I wouldn't get zabaglione at Timmi's Wine Bar.

Matt called for me before 8 a.m on the days I was in my own flat so that we could travel to work together. When I was staying with him, he let me stay in bed until the last minute, bringing me tea and toast. If it was raining, he brought out his golf umbrella. If the weather was really bad, he'd order a taxi to the underground. He left the tube himself at Temple, but I had two more stops to go. He'd squeeze my arm as he left, breathing in my ear. 'I'll collect you, as usual.'

And he did. Whatever time I left work, he'd be there. The others grinned at first. Later they just raised an eyebrow at him. Sometimes, someone would remark, 'No chance you slipping off for an evening shindig, then, Harriet!'

So we went to work together, we travelled back together. 'I really don't want to be without you a minute.' He wanted me to move in with him totally, but we decided that I'd keep on my flat. For tax reasons, that was best.

Early on, Matt ruled out marriage, tears in his eyes. He was already married. His poor wife, older than him, had early dementia and was in a care home. We used to visit her together. Since she didn't recognise him anymore, it wasn't hurtful for her to see him with a younger woman. In fact, she usually asked me, 'Are you my sister, dear?'

Matt explained that she didn't have a sister but that she had wanted one when she was little. 'So we're doing her a favour, visiting her together.'

The nursing staff assumed I was a sister and I left it at that.

If I went out, it was with Matt. We got invited as a couple. It was comforting to have him holding my arm, sitting by my side, suggesting what I might choose to eat, correcting any gaffe I made in conversation, sharpening up the tag line of any joke or anecdote I offered up. My chair was unfailingly pulled back before I sat down, the door opened for me, my coat cuddled round my shoulders before we went out into the cold.

It made me feel, for the first time in my life, that I was necessary, vital in fact. Matt would nuzzle my neck and murmur, 'You know I can't do without you, don't you?'

If I went food shopping while he was cooking he'd say, 'Don't be long.'

Of course, I miss all that, I do. But friends eventually made me wonder about myself. As we all left work and I made excuses, it would be, 'Harriet? Are you missing our Friday *again*? Aren't you a bit bored. I mean, he's quite old, too old for you.'

'You're becoming insular, Harriet. Always being a stop-at-home. Boring, boring.'

But then I'd feel superior as they conferred about who was booking a taxi, whether they needed coats, umbrellas, extra cash, before they went out. *I* would be met at the door, a large umbrella to protect my hair, a car parked near, a gin and tonic minutes away, a smile, a kiss, total acceptance. It was very cosy.'

I did wonder. Should I just let myself go like this? Shouldn't I have a life outside the Matt experience? But it was so much easier to let things be, and so comfortable.

It wasn't the office Christmas party that scotched it, always held on November 30th to ensure the firm did not pay peak date rates to the hotel or restaurant concerned. Yes, Matt stopped me going, sort of. He wasn't to know the date, he said, when he booked grand circle tickets for *Soft Magic*, the show that brought the West End to its feet (so *The Mail on Sunday* said). 'You wouldn't rather go to your work do, surely? Tasteless turkey and potatoes that aren't crisp, washed down with shop talk and the Argentinian house wine? I've managed to get hold of the two centre seats, second row. I know how you love your musicals.'

I had wanted to go to the office party, in fact. It could be a laugh, even if the food wasn't that special or the wine a good one. After you'd had a few, you didn't notice. I knew I'd feel out of it the next day when everyone was talking about what had happened. But then, Matt had bought the tickets. We couldn't waste those.

I began to feel rather down in the dumps.

It wasn't even the event of Christmas that caused a crisis. People say that is a stressful time but I found it very relaxing. We went to this luxurious mansion and had therapeutic treatments, two each day. I went home as passive as a fish in a hot lake and when Matt began to follow me in, I said, 'Too tired. I'm just going to flop out.'

He rang later, but I was too tired to answer the phone. It had been a luxurious Christmas. The next day we were due to visit his wife. I didn't want to. Mean of me, but it was a drag.

Then I picked up the latest Val McDermid novel, bought at the airport last year. How had I held off from this? Gripping? I'll say it was gripping.

While I was on my own, the girls came round and told me all the things they'd done over Christmas. I wanted to join in, have the same sort of stories, even the same males hanging around so we could swap notes. After describing the massages, I smiled and listened to the girls, but my heart had sunk to a level only my old mattress could reach.

Matt rang several times and I told him, 'I'm not sleeping well. I feel tired, too tired to go out, too tired to keep on going out with you. Don't come round, sorry, I'm tired.'

I stuck to my words, miserable though I was, snapping at people at work.

After weeks of my avoidance, Matt, always thoughtful, told me he'd ordered a mattress, that I needed a new one. Once I'd installed it, he urged, I'd start having good night's sleep and get my energy back. We'd go to the gym together, and return to our lovely evenings.

'Not,' I bellowed. His was only a voice message so I could be entirely rude to it.

I'd stopped answering the phone, so he had to email. *Good news for both of us, I think. The mattress will be delivered this Saturday.*

At least I wrote *thank you*, but that's all. I mean, a mattress doesn't sound exactly exciting (and I was wary of what he might mean by it.)

It's three days since my mattress arrived. Three wonderful nights. I can never look back. The phone's been nicely quiet. I'd disabled my voice messaging before the mattress even came, but I dreaded opening my emails.

There it was, the one from Matt. *Hello Harriet. Is it a good mattress? I think my wife missed you when I visited. She kept looking around me as if trying to see another person. You will come next time, won't you? Are you rested now? Shall I meet you at seven tomorrow, take you to that new musical? I can cook a beef Milanese for Sunday.*

I looked at my mattress and shook my head. I emailed him. *Sorry, no. It's over, Matt. I've found another support.*

The answer came straight back, as if his fingers had been hovering over the keys, ready. *I'll always be with you, make no mistake.*

I turned off the computer.

I haven't replied, and I'm not tired, and I don't want any beef Milanese. I'm not interested in a musical at the moment.

I've lain down, and the mattress seems to be rising up around me. Enveloped, totally relaxed, on my side, on my back, morning, noon or night, I know it will support me all ways. I turn my head; the mattress blocks my view. It has swollen like a hill on either side.

I think I'll prop my feet up a fraction. No, the mattress is rising gently at the bottom of the bed. They're supported. Perfect.

It's just so comfortable. I'll have to tell the girls how I really love my mattress. *Marrimatt*, that was its name, I remember now. Matt for short.

Is it my imagination or has it swollen further? Hadn't it reached full size after its first night? I can't see my arms; my matt is around them. My legs seem a long way from the rest of me, as if I'm on a cloud. I'm so lucky to be so supported.

I should get up now. The trouble is, I can't seem to clamber out . . .

I'll just turn over on to my back. Just for a while longer. So comfy, why move? I'll stay.

It's becoming too difficult to leave Matt behind.

A MATERIAL TRIP

Elaine sprinted the last few hundred yards, "Dmitri"s' footsteps echoing behind her. She got to the barrier just in time to see the tail end of the train disappear into the November mist. For some moments she stayed staring at the track, willing the train to miraculously reappear. She was only a few seconds too late but they could be the most significant seconds of her life. She turned on him, glaring. 'Now you see!'

He raised his shoulders with a rueful smile. 'Sorry.'

She hovered distractedly by the barrier hardly able to accept the situation. Her eyes searched the information display which confirmed that the 22:.18 was the last train of the day to Gatford. It wasn't that she didn't have the price of a night at some small hotel or a functioning mobile phone. It was that she could not now give Brian the explanation she had prepared. She could not get home tonight – so she couldn't go home at all.

She could just picture his heavy-jowled face, his narrowing eyes as she stumbled out an apology. There was no explanation he would believe so there was no point in staying in that life with him under a false accusation. If she'd been guilty that could be a different matter.

A day-return ticket to the London shops had represented a small break in her dull and restricted life with Brian. She'd been reaching for her handbag as he'd left scratching the back of his neck and reckoning that he might be home in time for dinner for once. On the train, the thought of browsing in High Street Ken, then trying on something silk in Liberty's had taken more time than the reading of *Glamour* magazine. But she hadn't even reached any shops, and now she couldn't get home either.

'It was the last train. I told you!' She hardly looked at her dark-eyed nemesis.

He came close to her side. 'Look – I didn't mean that happens.'

'Maybe, but you've caused this. Your outrageous escapade has caused this whole thing. You've changed my life and now you'll walk off with a shrug just the same as you were yesterday.'

He shuffled his feet but didn't move off. 'I not meaning anything, but best you come my place for the night.'

'Back to your place! After you forcibly held me nearly all day in that foul back room. All for the sake of your selfish criminal purposes.' It felt good to adopt the tone of an outraged heroine.

Before he answered, he looked at Elaine almost shyly. 'That not really my flat. Just safe holding place.'

'Safe for you! So you don't even own a flat? Or you stole that too while the owner was away? Or you have a better flat? Do I care? Do you really think I'll go anywhere with you willingly?'

'It's just that, you got no luggage and you perhaps shy booking into a hotel – a lady alone at this time of night.'

Elaine bit back a furious reply. He was right. Even though many women might come from a station needing a hotel, late at night, they'd have booked on their cell phone, have a briefcase at very least. Whatever, it would be embarrassing for her, never having done this before.

It might even be difficult to find a room. It would be no fun walking round the streets trying to find a vacancy. It would be easier at a smarter hotel but she was hardly dressed for it. Her clothes rang out 'cheap chain store', a state she'd intended to remedy by this shopping trip. What little confidence she'd had that morning, the small pale confidence connected with the predictability of her daily life, had been sharply eroded by the day's events.

She paused, looking at the ground. The litter of a normal busy day at Victoria station: wrappers, cigarette stubs, chewing gum, a comb, flakes of mud, demonstrated that other people had bought chocolate bars, had eaten them and been able to go on their way. They had gone to whatever shops they liked, drunk take-away coffee from a stall, they had approached their trains which they had caught and then travelled safely home, all as planned.

He proffered a hand. 'It's not as if I couldn't give you the money to stay over in comfort for as long as you like.'

She nearly choked on her anger. 'You think I would take it? The proceeds of other people's savings, now in your "safe holding place" along with the grime and dirty washing – a place stolen by you and used for my benefit? That makes me, present at the scene of the crime purely by accident, almost as guilty as you. People would think I'd helped plan the whole job.'

'Shh. Keep your voice down for f—, for the Lord's sake.' He looked around with some concern at the few night travellers. 'You talk like I been caught or something. I bonked the clerk from behind so when he comes round he can't give description. There weren't any witnesses.'

'Any *other* witnesses.'

'You won't go to police. Because you don't want explanations, interviews, hassle. You not going to shop me. We established that. That's why I let you go. It's our agreement. You're free because you helped me smuggle us out. It'd look like you in on it.'

She kicked a used cardboard cup out of the way. It was true. But it was also because she secretly liked him too much, the bastard. 'You'd have had to let me go sooner or later. You know you would. You're a petty burglar, not a murderer.'

'Robber. I'd never burgle! And I don't call £584,220 "petty".'

She paused. 'Jeeze! Is that what it came to?'

'Mmm. You could have a good life with that – there's enough.'

'It's enough to get a home with no mortgage,' she said with feeling. It was now nearly three years stuck in the one-bedroom unit that went with Brian's job, and it would still be a one-bedroom unit if he were promoted and transferred elsewhere, since they were childless. They had been saving, watching their nest egg grow at a pitiful pace – grow in the same building society as the one this loon had chosen to rob this morning.

'Thinking about it?' he said.

'Not in the way you mean.' She began walking away, knowing he would keep up, half wanting him to. Better not to be alone. London at past ten at night felt dangerous. She was unworldly, a Gatford girl, born and bred. Three hours from London on the one fast train of the day. It was enough of an adventure to go off to the West End shopping on her own in daylight. It had been quite enough of a new experience to be caught up in a robbery then hoisted off in a stranger's car. She had no wish to be roaming London, and not the best part of it either, late into the night.

"Dmitri" didn't feel like a threat now, not in comparison with the bundles in the doorways, mangy dogs beside them, or the brash, loud-voiced passers-by with their foreign accents and swinging raincoats. She looked up at him, the hard cheekbones, the dark, bold eyes, the gentle lips. He was hardly a stranger after she'd been cooped up with him all day with nothing else to look at.

At first, of course, she had been terrified. It was the shock of it, the speed. In the space of a few minutes after stepping inside the building society, she had seen a man on the floor unconscious, then been blindfolded before being rushed and pushed into a strange car with a gun poking into her as it jolted off.

She hadn't had time to adapt before she'd found herself in that horrible building when he'd pulled the blindfold off. He'd asked her basic questions: 'What your name, love?', and 'What time do they expect you home?'; 'Where you come from?' in a chatty manner with the gun steady in his hand.

'And your name is?' She wasn't going to be his victim.

'Dmitri. You can call me "Dmitri".'

She would, although it obviously wasn't his name. She hadn't heard of anyone called that since she had to study Shostakovich in college, and goodness knows how hard on the ears that was! But he probably did have a foreign name. He did look foreign.

He talked a lot to calm her down, quite a nice voice really although she couldn't agree with what he said.

'I know it's wrong but I'm not stealing from people, Elaine, I'm stealing from a bank. They'll make it up to their customers.'

'Building society. It's where people like me save their hard- earned money so they can buy a home one day.'

'They'll still be able to. The loss will go down to the bank, not to any of those people, don't worry.'

'It's still wrong.'

'I know, but I need a start. We need a lump sum.'

'We?'

'You'll see. Anyway, I'll stop thieving now if there's enough. Let me count it. I can if you sit still and stop giving me stick.'

His fingers were long. He licked one and turned each note delicately, mouthing the amounts to himself. He turned his back to her so that she couldn't see the number of piles, each one with a note folded round it. His back was curved and lean, not padded with lard like Brian's. His shoulder blades showed like wings under the folds of his shirt – not an expensive one but tasteful, checked, small check, green and navy, nice.

When he finished he shoved the lot into a paper bag, then turned. 'Good girl, you stayed still. I like that.' Then he made her tell him a bit more; where she'd been, who knew she was in London, exactly what she'd done before coming into the building society.

She was angry, resentful. 'My husband's working a long day today so I was going shopping. I was going to treat myself to some new clothes. I needed some money so I went into the building society first. No-one there but you in your camel coat, bent over a crumpled figure, poor man.

159

That's all I saw. Then you grabbed me, hustled me out down the alley with one arm behind my back. It still aches. Shoved me into your rotten van with a smelly hood over my face. That's where I've been. So I haven't done any of what I planned.'

'You look great when you're angry, you know that? All that marmalade hair bobbing around your face. You never screamed. I was glad of that.'

'Screaming isn't something I've ever had to do. It doesn't come naturally. I live a quiet life.'

He looked at her from under raven eyebrows. A rim of black eyelashes outlined his eyes. No, he wasn't English, she reckoned.

'You can live quiet life again. Provided you not give me away. Think what you gotta lose if you do, after being here with me all day.'

She shuddered but somehow he didn't seem dangerous. He was almost considerate, pulling out the chair for her, lighting the gas fire.

'Listen! My husband is expecting me to be at home when he finishes work. I was going to catch the 18:40. I still can, if you let me go.'

'We'll see. If I can trust you, we'll see.'

'They'll be after you already. Any minute now there'll be police at the door and you'll get a far worse sentence because you've kid-napped me.'

He turned to his paper bag of note rolls. 'I've finished counting. I go out to get you nice take-away. Just stay put, stay calm,' and he slid outside with his booty, locking the door quickly behind him. She certainly couldn't do any harm! There were only two wooden chairs, a bookcase and a carton with some cushions and saucepans on it. Otherwise the room was empty.

There was no TV, no radio. On the small bookcase were some volumes of poetry, modern poetry, a Tesco catalogue, an Argos catalogue and some paperbacks. She was too churned up to read any.

But then he was a long time, so she pulled two cushions on to the floor, leaned back on them and found herself surprisingly caught up by an Agatha Christie. That was what her grandmother had read, Agatha Christies. It was a good job Granny couldn't see her now.

When Dmitri came back she was almost glad to see him, as well as to smell fish and chips. It had been a very early start this morning. He escorted her to the bathroom. She saw the high window was only big enough for spiders to squeeze through. The towel on the rail looked clean. She hoped it was.

The fish and chips tasted good although she made sure she ate them with a bad grace. He'd also brought in tea, strong and in good but mismatching mugs. She turned one over. 'Royal Doulton? You stole these too?'

He didn't answer but didn't look guilty either. 'I dump the van, so we all right. Is natural you fed up with me. Can't expect much else from you at the moment.'

"At the moment" sounded ominous. What was coming next? She wouldn't ask.

It took the rest of the day to convince her that no shrilling siren would announce her rescue. By mid-afternoon, she was negotiating her release. He hadn't put a hand on her. She told him exactly what she thought and he didn't answer back, just looked at the floor but kept hold of his gun. It was more or less at the ready, but not actually pointing at her. She didn't even know if it was a real gun. She rummaged in her memory but felt fairly sure she had never actually seen a gun in real life before. It wasn't something her father would keep under his pile of *Practical Grocer* magazines.

She looked at Dmitri's long fingers and wondered he played an instrument and if it were he who had bought the poetry books – or a past lover, wife even. What emergency had turned him into a robber rather than a poet or a poet's husband? She had long stopped being frightened of him. She was far more involved with the inconvenience and complication of her situation. She was even rather bored.

She supposed he was sitting there thinking of his ways out, of what he'd say if stopped, of his cover. Lying would be run of the mill to him. He'd be working out what actions would be to his best advantage. Elaine just had to defer to his greater experience. All he needed was a bit of cooperation. She picked up the Agatha Christie again. Now there was a woman of infinite resources, someone clever at plotting, someone who always knew who was to blame.

Elaine reckoned she'd be a nuisance to Dmitri sooner or later. He'd have to let her go or . . . what? If Brian knew, there'd be trouble. Dmitri would be scared at the thought of her husband coming after her, outraged.

'Brian's going to know something's wrong straight away if I'm late, so you need to get things worked out so I can catch that train.'

'Keep calm, we have to wait till it's dark.'

The mechanics of their escape occupied him until well after dark. Elaine saw that her safety totally relied upon his. Their final emergence from the warehouse adjoining the flat was a joint effort managed through his planning and her cooperation, even a few extra ideas. The preoccupation then was to get to her train. Once on it, she could return home and pretend a theatre visit had delayed her, whilst Dmitri could slip quietly through the station away to whatever lair or treasure trove he kept. He was welcome to it.

She knew the last train went at 22:18 but was not sure how long it would take to get to Victoria. As long as she caught that train, she had a chance of returning to normality. She kept looking at her watch, willing him to get going.

'Don't worry, we'll make it,' Dmitri said. 'You'll be free of me then.'

And eventually they did go, his hand grasping her arm fiercely, his gun pressed into her side. She didn't recognize where they were. It certainly wasn't the West End. It was a long walk down lots of dingy small streets before they came to a main road. She'd never recognize any of it again. They got to a bus stop.

'No car then?'

'And you record the number plate? No way.'

He pushed her into a seat behind the driver where she could see very little. By the time they were sitting anonymously on the crowded bus, despite the gun pressed into her hip, Elaine felt a sense of jubilation as much as relief. It was almost as if she had planned and successfully carried out a crime herself.

The number of bus stops seemed interminable.

'This plodding bus! It'll be curtains if I don't make that train.'

'Calm down. We're nearly there.'

They were both at the door by the time the bus reached the station. Elaine was so relieved and eager that her arm eluded his grasp. They both ran hard. The sight of Brian's face would never be so welcome once she got home. It was only as Elaine saw the train draw away that she recognized her life had irrevocably changed.

The train, the one means of late night travel to Gatford, had gone and with it the only plausible excuses that would have made her return possible. In the morning, Brian wouldn't believe her story. That was his training. She'd have to give him chapter and verse. He'd suspect the worst and he wouldn't accept he was wrong.

Telling Brian what had really happened would mean opening the whole embarrassing, demeaning incident to everyone for a full examination. Even the newspapers would be interested. Imagine having her photograph in the local news! And if Brian didn't believe her, who else would? She would have to explain to the office why she wasn't at work. They'd snigger behind her back, assuming some dirty assignation. Everyone would want to know every last detail instead of the whole thing being closed off and, if she could manage it, forgotten.

Elaine looked around the station. The ordinary night-time closing down operations were the beginning of her new life. Life with nothing but a handbag. She would have to go to the temp agency in the morning, take the first job offered. But where would she spend the night?

Her companion broke into her thoughts. 'You could stay at the station hotel without luggage. They'll be used to it. After all, it's true you missed your train. You wouldn't have to pretend. In the morning, you can go back. Safe and sound. No hassle.'

She explained the situation she'd be in with Brian, using her most irritated voice.

'If I was married,' he said, 'my wife would be able to tell me everything and I'd trust her.'

So he wasn't married.

'And if she didn't want me to tell anyone else, I wouldn't.'

'It's different for you. In your life people probably don't ask questions, unless they're kidnapped. Like me. And the more I answer questions, the more what I *think* I am seems different from what it is, or what they want or think it should be. Oh you won't understand.'

Elaine broke off in frustration. 'You don't know me.'

'How many other people have you spent a whole day with since you got married?'

'None of course.' She hadn't thought of this before, but it was true. After marriage, you only ever saw bits of people for bits of time.

'Right. So you see I'm someone you know pretty well. Now we must meet in nicer circumstances.'

'Why on earth should we? Haven't you foisted yourself on me for long enough?'

He pulled down his hat. It had a brim, shading his face. It looked very smart. So did the camel coat. He was the smart one, not Elaine.

He said, 'I think I'll stay over at the hotel myself. I'm some way from my place.'

'You don't live in that dump by the warehouse then?'

'Bless saints, no. So I'll stay over. You get fewer funny looks if you with me. Oh, don't worry, don't worry, we can have separate rooms. You can be my sister. There has to be good reason why I'm paying your bill.'

She stayed still but he took her arm and led her gently toward the station hotel. As he drew her nearer to him she could feel the wadge of notes beneath his coat.

'I never asked you your real name,' she said.

'Does it matter? What would you like me to be called? No obscenities if you please.'

She looked at him. 'Is it Douglas?'

'Suits me. Douglas—' he looked up at a nearby poster, 'Winchester. How do you do. Now we are fully introduced. You can be Miss Elaine Winchester, secretary.'

'I am a secretary, actually. Well, data clerk to be exact.'

'And your old man?'

'Police constable. Waiting promotion. We live in a police flat.' She spoke the words viciously. It would be too much to hope for that he would shake with fear or something. In any case, her expression probably summoned up the small flat, lonely nights, anxieties, uncertain hours; the dinginess of her life. She didn't need to describe the brakes on her conversation, on her friendships outside of work.

'Oh, I see,' he said.

'Yes. From policeman's wife to criminal's accomplice, all in one day.' It felt depressing more than worrying.

Warmth hit them as he ushered her towards the welcoming lights of the hotel foyer. He swanned up to the booking clerk and booked the two rooms. He asked about food. The dining room was closed but room service was available. He ordered for both of them, confident enough not to ask Elaine's opinion. She was past caring what she ate, if she ate.

'I'll need to telephone.'

'Sorry I had to chuck your mobile. There will be telephones in the bedrooms. You can phone your old man upstairs.'

She led the way.

He removed the phone from her room and had her ring from his room, his index finger hovering over the button in case she dialled the police. Afterwards she shut the door of the bathroom on him and only came out when he knocked to say that Room Service had brought their meals.

'Well, what he say, what he say?' he pressed her, as he passed her the tray.

'No reply.' She sucked in her cheeks to prevent her smile forming. 'He must've been wanted at the station. He often is. Emergency, someone not turned up for the night duty, extra men needed for a pub riot. Who knows?'

He paused. Then he countered: 'So you could go back in the morning. Shopping in town, staying with an aunt, missing your train, held up by a robber, where you been? Who knows?'

Elaine looked at his chiselled cheek bones, the angle of his chin, his dark, promising eyes. '*I* know, Douglas. That's who.' She put her coat on a hanger and sat down by the tray of mushroom risotto.

His lean face creased into a smile of rare sunshine. 'Having you here, this is bliss for me you know.' He raised his glass but she just drank, quite deeply.

After she'd eaten her fill she gave him the full benefit of her steady gaze. 'You can't stick a gun into my side every moment of every day. You've got a choice. Either give all that money back and I'll stay with you, or keep the money and escape right now. Leave me enough to get a taxi all the way home, and I'll go right away. It might be fifty pounds or much more, but what'd be that be to you?'

She stood up with a confident disdain new to her, her hand on her British Home Stores anorak. A more comfortable life might well be ahead. She might not know his real name but it felt really good to be giving some man a Hobson's choice.

She stuck her chin in the air. 'Well? What's it to be? My taxi fare or return the whole lot?'

He pulled the huge wadge of notes from his coat pocket and put the entire roll onto the bed.

'There you are. *You* choose, Elaine.'

WELL WOMAN

The Guardian had a special offer. *Well Woman Examination*, normally for a figure totally out of my reach. With the offer, reachable.

When I applied, I learned the private hospital I had to attend was quite a drive. That only mattered because of the stipulation: nothing to eat or drink after seven in the evening. As if having your innards and outers thoroughly gone into by a strange doctor wasn't enough, I'd have to be starved and dehydrated first.

Emptily, I drove to the poplar-lined avenue where the hospital stood well back from the road, fronted by flower-filled borders and a curved, gravelled drive. Parking in front of the stately building was a breeze. A generous area invited Day Patients. I climbed the low-rise steps to the heavily embossed door. Beyond it, a smiling receptionist with a twenty-three-inch waist and a pretty blouse behind the tiniest of desks rose to her feet. The reception hall was magnificent in magnolia and the calmest of greens. I was welcomed like the most esteemed guest.

Into the William Morris papered hallway, and a doorway opened. The politest of nurses appeared to usher me into an ante-chamber. She allowed me to undress at my leisure, an immaculate gown laid out ready for me on a couch.

She then led me into the consulting room with its garden-view windows to meet the doctor, a Bond Street stripe just showing under his well-fitting white coat.

The nurse stood aside, ready. The only thing between me and a total lack of dignity was a white gown. Since it was open down the back that was only a gesture for fronting the world, like a Venetian mask. Once removed, the difference in status between masked, unmasked, clothed, unclothed was only too clear. I knew my place, I stood and listened.

The doctor wanted everything, far more than a demanding lover. I had to donate my outer, my inner, my blood, my mucus, my urine, my faeces.

I submitted. Then I answered all the questions obediently. Passing examinations was no new thing for me.

Eventually it was over. The doctor ushered me from the room and the nurse followed.

The nurse said in a kind voice that she was getting me tea and toast. This was a private examination after all. Following it, you were to be nurtured before the doctor returned with printouts, analyses and advice or really bad news.

Meanwhile I was left alone to dress. How welcome the privacy of the cubicle with its white surrounding curtains. I was protected on all four sides, a welcome contrast to the threatening open flap at my back. I slipped on my all-around garments and put the gown on the door, open side out to warn the next patient.

Time for me to do the examining. I was in a cell, really: black easy-clean examination couch, pale- blue blanket, paper undersheet, screen, hard chair, sink, taps, rubber gloves, glass jar, and receiving dish, kidney shaped.

I put my shoes on. After dressing, what was there to do?

The nurse was a very long time returning. It was eighteen hours since I'd eaten, only water being allowed. It's not a drink I'm used to, no kick to it.

I hadn't brought a book. Usually I have at least travel leaflets in my bag, *'What to do in Walsall'* or *'Places of Interest in Inverness,'* but not today, not. I looked around. There was nothing to do or look at. Not so much as a biological diagram. There wasn't even a design on the curtains. The rubber gloves were too big to try on and anyway, I thought they might have been used.

The only other objects present were two bins, one labelled *Chemical Waste,* the other, *Waste.*

I have a boredom problem. I opened the bins.

"Chemical Waste" had nasty things with phials and needles and soggy bandages. "Waste" was more interesting and produced treasure – a cellophane pack marked *Prosthesis* sat near the top.

I extracted it quickly, tore open its cover and sat squeezing its impossible pinkness, full of tiny holes like Maltesers, a very squashy thing ideal for stress reduction. It was smooth and it was bouncy, leaping back after finger pressure. I squeezed it as hard as I could into the ball of my palm. I pressed in my thumbs. I patted its curve. I began to see why men like boobs. I loved my prosthesis, and hid it in my bag when my tea and toast came. The warm toast just the right crispness, a little white dish with plenty of butter, another with Cooper's marmalade.

I must say the quality of both tea and toast far surpasses the usual hospital café. There really does seem to be a point in going private.

After this treat I felt much better, so that when I went into the consulting room to sit behind the large mahogany partners' desk with its brass lamp and droop-proof orchid, I sat back comfortably to hear the doctor's verdict, my hands hidden in my bag, squeezing away at my prosthesis.

I heard something about tests taken and a test reviewed, but forget what else the doctor said. I'm sure it was important. Anyway, he said he would post a report on to me.

At the door I asked, 'Did you say I needed a breast removed?' He looked at me as if I were mad. (I am rather flat-chested).

'My dear Mrs Woodbury, that's the last thing you need. Whatever made you worry about that?'

That meant my prosthesis was illicit property, but I've kept it handy anyway. No man will ever enjoy its charms, but it's reduced so much of my stress.

I've told everyone I know that they'll profit from a well woman visit.

ANTI-DOTE

In the beginning, when light shone in her eyes and vigour marked her step, she knew above all how much he loved her, how special she was.

'It's not just that,' he murmured.

Deep in the green of his irises the tiny cubes of light reflected the bounce of her curls, her cherubic chin, the turn of her cheek, pink with the devotion of her lover.

'You are the apple of my eye,' he said, never afraid to be unoriginal or sentimental. 'You are the love of my life. I adore you. I would be lost without you.'

Quite clearly no-one around matched her. She glowed and glistened and turned her adorable head, confident to step into the world, a little this way, a little that way, not a lot, for why would she need to?

'I want to share the rest of my life with you, and only with you,' he said.

And so he did.

Without thinking it through, she had expected bliss. She had the right to expect bliss. Bliss? Certainly there was her double-rack wardrobe in its own little room, a music centre with the latest technology and neighbours too far away to be a nuisance. She could return at night so late it was morning; a Teasmaid sat beside the mammoth marital bed.

In the kitchen stood a dresser filled with so many dishes that washing up never entered her days. An older lady with tree- trunk legs and no make-up tidied and cleaned the home. The lovely home: a cream drawing room with door-sized windows, an ivory plush chaise longue and a verdant view of a landscaped garden she did not have to tend.

Her mother breathed, 'You are the mistress of this— universe. You have achieved everything, not the others, just you. You're a girl who just has a certain something . . . that *that*. Oh, no other word for it,' her mother exulted, the first and last time she was asked to visit them.

So she had *that*. It was a good feeling.

In the evenings he would return, allowing her daytime pastimes and breathing admiration. 'You are the most wonderful thing. I feel I have dreamed you up. I want nothing for you but bliss.'

Lying in a gown of sapphire, extending a finger with a ring to match, she touched a bell. It brought marrons glacés and petits fours balanced one-handed by a young girl bestowed with deference and a suitably poor complexion. This was bliss, wasn't it?

The house held hobby rooms and health equipment, a sauna and jacuzzi. Even the kitchen was a seduction to leisure activity; its black marble counters, islands for concocting delicacies, technology at its sweetest. Nothing had been denied her, special woman that she was. Her man had demonstrated his devotion.

Even so, over time, there were moments when his deficiencies caused him to act in ways that hurt her. If her boeuf en croute appeared crusty or carbonned, sharp words left his imperfect lips as cinders splutter from a damp fire. She knew the patient caste of her face was irresistible. It was important not to let any emotions allow lines to form on her skin. She always checked her expressions in the oval mirror, its gold curlicued frame a suitable decorative surround for its subject.

Days and months and years passed. She was not without pleasure, but was she in bliss? She had occasional suspicions that he was not making the most of her charms. It was sad that he was missing out on these delights. Sometimes she wondered at his slowness to respond with the actions the world would expect: caresses, exclamations, songs of praise.

'You have forgotten to kiss me this evening!' Then of course he did. But having to be reminded! Such guilt he must suffer for his inadequacies. Accordingly, she showed such kindness in her economy of criticism. Beauty, she told herself, comes from within. The weight of his debt to her must be distressing.

Years on, the mirror on the bedroom wall, so brightly filled with sunrise in days past, began to mist to beige. She would move closer to catch the glint of her genius but somehow it escaped her. He must replace this mirror; it had outlived its time.

In the evenings she came close to him, breathily close, and waited for him to wilt with desire. At times she caught him out and managed to come and go from his presence without his realizing it.

At other times, allowing him to listen to her, to enjoy the rise and fall of her treble and tenor, she noticed his eyelids droop. He had a poor energy level – he was not a perfect specimen of manhood. There were times now when she had not felt exultant for days, perhaps weeks. Surely his short-comings were not making her change?

After a day when she had admitted her intention of visiting her mother, which would mean abandoning him for an entire week to visit on her own, and he had merely responded, 'Oh yes . . .' and hadn't shown a need for consolation or explanation, she found herself upstairs without her floral blouse and crêpe de chine lingerie, searching for her peach bloom, her strokeable body, her flush of youth. It was worrying that the bathroom mirror could not capture her allure any better than that dulling mirror in the bedroom. Where was the light of day? She listened for the sweetness of her breathing; her fingertips searched for her svelte shape and silken texture.

She tripped downstairs just as she was, to stand in front of him, silent, so that he could discover the woman he had shown her, known her to be. He was reading his spreadsheets. He didn't look up until she coughed. Was he blinded by the glare of the August sun, its beams translated through the nine-foot window onto her displayed body? She changed her pose. She saw his eyes upon her. She waited.

His eyes, once the colour of fresh apple, were like strained tea. She saw that he looked without seeing. He did look, didn't he?

She looked instead – up herself and down herself – as the sun glowed and lowered its gleam to fall upon the pale Chinese carpet. Her body sensed the warmth of the sun leaving her with its last glance of gold, rust and mahogany.

She saw the image the sun had left behind.

Bliss, if there it ever had been, was gone with the sun to shine towards another world.

Then she saw her sunless self. She was beige and she was crinkled, a square and emptied shape outlining where his hopes and dreams had lain. She had become like a brown paper bag without its apples.

She was a paper bag. A bag. Of course – she always had been. It was a myth that she had ever been a woman.

That she ever had been.

That she ever had.

That she ever.

That she.

That.

THE END

TO THE READER

(Poor Bellissima - or was she originally Maureen or Dot?)

If you have enjoyed *Me-Time Tales*, please consider leaving a review on Goodreads and/or Amazon. This helps guide prospective readers, and authors really appreciate their reviewers' time.

In the course of time, the curious men may emerge to furnish a book of their own. Keep an eye open for a collection of quirky stories entitled Curious Men. Who knows who or what will feature inside - maybe a consort of one of the (more or less) mature women from the Me-Time Tales?

See overleaf for other (very different) books by Rosalind Minett:

A RELATIVE INVASION
A trilogy set in 1937-1959
Book 1: Intrusion
Book 2: Infiltration
Book 3: Impact (forthcoming)

CRIME SHORTS: e book series.
1. A boy with potential
2. Homed: who's guilty child or adult?
3. Not Her Fault.
And more sinfulness coming your way.

See all the books on the Amazon Rosalind Minett page:
http://www.amazon.co.uk/Rosalind-Minett/e/B00J5LZXLG

Rosalind blogs at www.characterfulwriter.com
where you can sign up to receive her newsletter.